Falling for the Rebel Princess

Ellie Darkins

ISBN-13: 978-0-373-74434-3

Falling for the Rebel Princess

First North American Publication 2017

This edition published by arrangement with Harlequin Books S.A.

For questions and comments about the quality of this book, please contact us at CustomerService@Harlequin.com.

HARLEQUIN®
www.Harlequin.com

Printed in U.S.A.

Ellie Darkins spent her formative years devouring romance novels, and after completing her English degree she decided to make a living from her love of books. As a writer and editor her work now entails dreaming up romantic proposals, hot dates with alpha males and trips to the past with dashing heroes. When she's not working she can usually be found running around after her toddler, volunteering at her local library, or escaping all the above with a good book and a vanilla latte.

Books by Ellie Darkins

Harlequin Romance

Frozen Heart, Melting Kiss
Bound by a Baby Bump
Newborn on Her Doorstep
Holiday with the Mystery Italian

Visit the Author Profile page
at Harlequin.com for more titles.

For Mike and Matilda

CHAPTER ONE

'NOT YET!' CHARLIE GASPED, willing herself to be dragged back under.

In her dream her skin was hot and damp, on fire from his touch.

Awake, her tongue felt furry.

In her dream her body hummed, desperate for the feel of him.

Awake, her eyes stung as she peeled them open.

In her dream she begged for more, and got everything she didn't even know she needed.

Awake, she needed to pee.

She admitted defeat and stretched herself properly alive, wincing at the harsh Nevada sunlight assaulting her in the hotel room. As her toes encountered skin she flinched back, realising that she did have this one, small reminder of her dream. The man who'd taken the starring role was beside her on the mattress, his face turned away from her, his arms and legs sprawled and caught in the sheets. She looked away. She couldn't think about him. Not yet.

Easing herself out of bed, she willed him not to wake. And worked her thumb into her waistband, rubbing at her skin where her jeans had left a tight red line. The T-shirt she'd slept in was twisted and creased, and she glanced around the room, wondering whether her luggage had been transferred when the hotel had upgraded them to a luxury suite. She shuddered when she caught sight of herself in the mirror and tried to pull her hair up into some sort of order.

It had started out backcombed and messy, and her eyeliner had never been subtle in her life—but a couple of hours' sleep had taken the look from grunge to tragic. She wiped under her eyes with a finger, and the tacky drag of her skin made her shudder. And desperate to shower.

A glint of gold caught her eye and stopped her dead.

No. That had been the dream. It had to be.

She went over her memories, rooted to the spot, staring at the ring, trying to pull apart what was dream and what was real. After eighteen hours travelling and many more without sleep, the past twenty-four hours barely felt real, images and memories played through her mind as if they had happened to somebody else.

The thrumming, heaving energy of the gig last night. That was real. The music capturing her senses, hijacking her emotions and pumping her full of adrenaline. Real.

Hot and sweaty caresses just before dawn. Dream.

Dancing with Joe in the club, trying to talk business, shouting in his ear. Moving so closely with him that they felt like one body. Feeling the music play between them like a language only they spoke. Maybe that was real.

The slide of his bare skin against hers. So, so dreamy.

Him talking softly as they lay on the bed, trading playlists on their phones, sharing a pair of headphones, until one and then both of them fell asleep. God, she wished she knew.

But as she raised her left hand and examined the demure gold band on her third finger, she was certain of one thing.

Vegas chapel wedding. Real.

She banged her head back against the wall. Why did she always do this? She was losing count of the number of times she'd looked over the wreckage of her life after one stupid, impulsive move after another and wished that she could turn back time. If she had the balls to go home and tell her parents that she didn't want their royal way of life and everything that came with it, maybe she'd stop hitting the self-destruct button. But starting that conversation would lead to questions that she'd never be prepared to answer.

Thinking back to the night before, she tried to remember what had triggered her reaction. And then she caught sight of the newspaper, abandoned beside the bed. The slip of the paper under her fingertips made her shiver with the memory of being handed one like it backstage in the club last night, and she let out a low groan. It had been the headline on the front page: Duke Philippe bragging about his forthcoming engagement to Princess Caroline Mary Beatrice of Afland, otherwise known as Charlie. It was the sort of match her parents had been not so subtly pushing on her for years, the one she was hoping that would go away if she ignored it for long enough. She knew unequivocally that she would never marry, and especially not someone like Duke Philippe.

She'd left the cold, rocky, North Sea island of Afland nearly ten years ago, when she'd headed to London determined to make her own way in the music business. Her parents had given her ten years to pursue her rebellion—as they put it. But they all knew what was expected after that: a return to Afland, official royal duties, and a practical and sensible engagement to a practical, sensible aristocrat.

So there was nothing but disappointment in store for her family, and for her.

She shrank into the bathroom and hid the newspaper as she heard stirring from the bed. Perhaps if she hid for long enough it just wouldn't be true—Joe Kavanagh and their marriage would fade away as the figment of her imagination that she knew they must be.

Marriage. She scoffed. This wasn't a marriage. It was a mistake.

But it seemed as if her body didn't care which bits of last night were real and which were imagined. The hair on her arms was standing on end, her heart had started to race, and she felt a yearning deep in her stomach that seemed somehow familiar.

'Morning,' she heard Joe call from the bedroom, and she wondered if he'd guessed that she was hiding out in there. 'I know you're in there.'

The sound of his voice sent another shiver of recognition. British, and educated. But there was also a burr of something rugged about it, part of his northern upbringing that felt exotically 'authentic', when compared to the marble halls and polished accents of her childhood.

She risked peeking round the bathroom door and mumbled a good morning, wondering why she hadn't just left the minute that she'd woken up—running had always worked for her before. She'd been running from one catastrophe to another for as long as she could remember. Because this was her suite, she reminded herself. They'd been upgraded when the manager of the hotel had heard about their impromptu wedding, and realised that he had royalty and music royalty spending their wedding night in his hotel.

The only constant in her life since she'd left the palace in Afland had been her job. She'd worked from the bottom of the career ladder up to her position as an A&R executive, signing bands for an independent record label, Avalon.

And that was the reason she had to get herself out of this room and face her new husband. Because not only was he a veritable rock god, he was also the artist that she'd been flown out here to charm, persuade and impress with her consummate professionalism in a last-ditch bid to get him to sign with her company.

She held her head high as she walked back into the bedroom, determined not to show him her feelings. The sun was coming in strong through the windows, and the backlighting meant that she couldn't quite see his expression.

'How's the head?' he asked, his expression changing to concerned.

She wondered whether she should tell him that she'd only had a couple of beers at most last night. That her recklessness hadn't come from alcohol, it had been fuelled by adrenaline and something more dangerous—the destructive path she found herself on all too often whenever marriage and family and the future entered the conversation.

Had Joe been drunk last night? She didn't think so. He'd seemed high when he'd come off stage, but she had been at enough gigs to know the difference between adrenaline and something less legal. She remembered him necking a beer, but that was it. So he didn't have that excuse either.

Why in God's name had this ever seemed like a good idea—to either of them?

'I've felt better,' she admitted, crossing the room to perch on the edge of the bed.

Up close, she decided that it really wasn't fair that he looked like this. His hair was artfully mussed by the pillows, his shirt was rumpled, and his tiny hint of eyeliner had smudged, but the whole look was so unforgivably sexy she almost forgot that whatever had happened the night before had been a huge mistake.

But sexy wasn't why she'd married him. Or maybe it was. When she went into reckless self-destruction mode, who was to say why she did anything?

Even in this oasis in the middle of the desert, she hadn't been able to escape the baggage that came with being a member of the royal family. The media obsession with royal women marrying and reproducing. Someone had raised a toast when they had seen her, to her impending marriage, asked her if she was up the duff and handed her a bottle of champagne. She'd been tempted to down the whole thing without taking a breath, determined to silence the voices in her head.

'So,' she said. 'I guess we're in trouble.'

Trouble? She was right about that. Everything about this woman said trouble. He had known it the minute that he had set eyes on her, all attitude and eyeliner. He had known it for sure when they'd started dancing, her body moving in time with his. So at what point last night had trouble seemed like such a good idea?

When they'd left the dance floor, in that last club, their bodies hot and sticky. When she'd been trying to talk business but he'd been distracted by the humming of his skin and the sparks that leapt from his body to hers whenever she was near. When Ricky, the drummer in his band, had joked that he needed to show some real rock-star behaviour if they were going to sell the new album, and Joe had dropped to one knee and proposed.

He hadn't thought for a second that she would go along with it.

But Charlie had stopped for a moment as their eyes had met, and as everyone had laughed around them he had been able to see that she wasn't laughing, and neither was he.

The club had stilled and quietened, or maybe it was just his mind that had, but suddenly there had been just the two of them, connected through something bigger than either of their bodies could contain. Something he couldn't pretend to comprehend, but that he knew meant that they understood each other.

And then she had nodded, thrown back her head and laughed along with everyone else, and they had been carried on a wave of adrenaline, bonhomie and contagious intoxication into a cab and up the steps of the courthouse. Somehow, still high from their performance and bewitched by the Princess, he hadn't stepped out of their fantasy and broken the spell.

They'd been cocooned in that buzz, carrying them straight through the ceremony. Such a laugh as they'd toppled out of the chapel. Right up until that kiss. Then it had all felt very real.

Did she remember that feeling as they had kissed for the first time? He knew in his bones that he could never forget it, as they were pronounced husband and wife.

'Are you going to hide in there all morning?' he asked.

In the daylight, she didn't look like a princess any more than she had the night before. Maybe that was how he'd found himself here. He'd expected to be on edge around her, but as soon as he had met her… Not that he was relaxed—no, there was too much going on, too much churning and yearning and *desire* to call it relaxed. But he'd been… He wasn't sure of the word. Her boss had sent her out here to convince him that their label was a good fit—and he'd been right. They had… Maybe fit was the right world. They'd just understood each other. She understood the music. Understood him. And when they had started dancing, there had been no question in his mind that this was important. He didn't know what it was, but he knew that he wanted more.

And marrying her—it had been a good move for the band. You couldn't buy publicity like that. He must have been thinking about that, must have calculated this as a business move. It was the only thing that made sense.

But was she expecting a marriage?

Because she came with a hell of a lot of baggage. Oh, he knew which fork to use, and how to spot the nasty ones in a room of over-privileged Henrys. He'd learned that much at his exclusive public school, where his music scholarship had taken him fee-free. But the most important part of his education had been the invaluable lesson he'd got in his last year—everyone was out to get something, so you'd better work out what you wanted in return.

The only place he felt relaxed these days was on the road, with his band. They moved from city to city, sometimes settling for a few weeks if they could hire some studio space, otherwise going from gig to gig, and woman to woman, without looking back. Everyone knowing exactly what they wanted, and taking what was on offer with no strings attached.

'Come on,' he said, reaching for her hand. As his fingertips touched hers he had another flash of that feeling from last night. The electric current that had joined them together as they had danced; that had woven such a spell around them that even a visit to a courthouse hadn't broken it.

'I can't believe we got married. This was your fault. Your idea.'

Was she for real? He shrugged and reminded her of the details. 'No one forced you. You seemed to think it was a great idea last night.'

So why was she looking at her ring as if it were burning her?

'Wh...?'

He waited to see which question was burning uppermost in her mind.

'Why? Why in God's name did I think it was a great idea?'

'How am I supposed to know if you don't? Maybe you were thinking it would be good publicity for the album.'

He looked at her carefully. Yes, that was why they had done it. But also...no. There was more to it. He couldn't believe that she was such a stranger this morning. When they'd laughed about this last night, it hadn't just been a publicity stunt—that sounded too cold. It had been a joke, a deal, between friends. A publicity stunt was business, but last night, as they'd laughed together on the way to the courthouse, it had been more than that.

And maybe that was where he had gone wrong, because he knew how this worked. He knew that all relationships were deals, with each partner out to get what they wanted. He had no reason to be offended that she was acting like that this morning.

'I'm not sure why you're mad at me. You thought it was a great idea last night.'

'I hadn't slept for thirty-six hours, Joe. I

think we can say that I wasn't doing my best reasoning. We have to undo this. What are my parents going to say?'

Her parents, the Queen of Afland and her husband. He groaned inwardly.

'Last night you said, and I quote, "They're going to go mental." As far as I could work out, that was a point in the plan's favour.'

In the cold light of morning—not such a good idea. Bad, in fact. Very bad.

He had married a princess—an actual blue-blooded, heir-to-the-throne, her-mother's-a-queen *princess*.

He was royally screwed.

'Look,' Joe said. 'I'm hungry, too hungry to talk about this now. How about we go out for breakfast and discuss this with coffee and as much protein as they can cram on a plate?'

CHAPTER TWO

CHARLIE GAZED INTO her black coffee, hoping that it would supply answers. Her memories had started to filter back in as she'd sipped her first cup; shame had started creeping in with her second. She hoped that this cup, her third, would be the one that made her feel human again.

'So how do we undo this?' she said bluntly. 'This is Vegas. They must annul almost as many marriages as they make here. Do we need to go back to the courthouse?'

She looked up and met Joe's eye. He was watching her intently as he took a bite of another slice of toast. 'We could,' he said. 'If we want an annulment, I guess that's how we go about it.'

'If?' She nearly spat out her coffee. 'I don't think you understand, Joe. We got *married*.'

'I know: I was there.'

'Am I missing something? The way I see things, we were joking around, we thought it would be hil*ar*ious to have a Vegas wedding, and we've woken up this morning to a major disaster. Aren't you interested in damage limitation?'

'Of course I am, but, unlike you, I think the reasons we got married were sound. Not necessarily the *best* reasons to enter into a legally binding personal commitment, but sound nonetheless.'

She raised her eyebrows. 'Remind me.'

'Okay, obvious ones first. Publicity. The band needs it. The album is almost finished, we're looking for a new label, and there is no such thing as bad publicity, right?'

'Mercenary much?'

'Look, this isn't my fault. You were good with mercenary last night.'

She snorted. 'Fine, publicity is one reason. Give me another.'

'It shows you're serious about the band.'

She crossed her arms and sat back in her seat, fixing him with a glare. 'I've signed plenty of bands before without marrying the lead singer. They signed with me because they trust that I'm bloody good at my job. Are you seriously telling me that whether or not I would marry you was going to be a deal-breaker?'

He leaned forward, not put off by her death stare. In fact, his eyes softened as he reached for her hand, pulling her back towards him. She went with it, not wanting to look childish by batting him away.

'Of course it wasn't,' he said gently. 'But breaking the marriage now? I'm not sure how that's going to play out. I'm not sure what our working relationship could look like with that all over the papers.'

She shook her head, looking back into the depths of her coffee, still begging it for answers.

'All of which I have to weigh against the heartbreak of my family if we don't bury this right now.'

She avoided eye contact as she tried to stop the tears from escaping. But she took a deep breath and when she looked up they were gone. 'Do you think anyone knows already? The press?'

'We weren't exactly discreet,' he said, with a sympathetic smile. 'I'd think it's likely.'

'And that can't be undone, annulment or not.'

He leaned back and took a long drink of his orange juice. 'So let's control the narrative.'

'What do you mean?'

'What story would hurt your family more—a whirlwind romance and hasty Vegas marriage, or a drunken publicity stunt to further your career? Because that's how the tabloids are going to want to spin it.'

'What's your point, Joe?' She'd taken her hand back and crossed her arms again, sure that this conversation was taking a turn that she wasn't going to like.

'All I'm saying is that we can't go back in time. We can't get unmarried, whether we get an annulment or not. So we either dissolve the marriage today and deal with the fallout to our reputations…'

'Or…?'

'Or we stay married.'

Her breathing caught as just for a second she considered what that might mean, to be this man's wife.

'But we're not in love. Anyone's going to be able to see that.'

He scrutinised her from under his lashes, which were truly longer and thicker than any man's had a right to be. 'So we're going to have to work hard to convince them. You can't deny that it's a better story.'

'And you can't deny that it means lying to my family. Ruining all the plans they were making for my life. I don't know what your relationship with your family is like, but I'm not sure that I can pull it off. I'm not sure that I want to. Things are diffi—'

She stopped before she revealed too much. Joe raised an eyebrow, obviously curious about why she had cut herself off, but he didn't push her on it.

'Would you rather they knew the truth?'

Of course not. She had been hiding the truth from them for years, ever since she'd found out that she could never be the daughter or the Princess that they needed her to be.

'Are we seriously having this conversation? You want to stay married? You do know that you're a rock star, right? If you were that desperate for publicity you could have found a hundred girls who actually *wanted* to be your wife.'

'Wow, you're quite something for a guy's ego. For the record, this isn't some elaborate ruse to get myself a woman. I don't have any problems on that score. All I'm doing is making the best of a situation. That's all.'

Charlie took a big bite of pie, hoping that the sugar would succeed where the coffee hadn't.

'Well, I'm glad to hear that you're not remotely interested in me as a woman.'

He fixed her with a meaningful stare, the intensity of his expression making it impossible for her to look away.

'I never said that.'

Heat rose in her belly as he held the eye contact, leaving her in no doubt about how he thought of her. She shook her head as he finally broke the contact. 'I can't believe that I'm even considering this. You're crazy. There's no way we can keep this up. What happens if we slip? What happens when someone finds out it's not for real? What happens when one of us meets someone and this marriage of convenience isn't so convenient any more?'

He reached for her hand across the table, and once again there was that crackle, that spark that she remembered from the night before. She saw him in the chapel, eyes creased in laughter, as he leaned in to kiss her. Those eyes were still in front of her, concerned now though, rather than amused.

'It doesn't have to be for ever. Just long enough that it doesn't look like a stunt when we split. You weren't planning on marrying someone else any time soon, were you?'

'Never.' Her coffee cup rattled onto the saucer with a clash, liquid spilling over the top.

'Wow—that really was a no.'

She locked her gaze on his—he had to understand this if they were going to go on. 'I mean it, Joe. I didn't want to get married. Ever. I'm not wife material.'

'And yet here I am, married to you.'

He held her gaze and there was something familiar there. Something that made her stomach tighten in a knot and her skin prickle in awareness. With all the unexpected drama of finding themselves married, it seemed as if they'd both temporarily forgotten that they had also found themselves in bed together that morning.

Perhaps he was remembering something similar, because all of a sudden there was a new fire in his eyes, a new heat in the way that he was looking at her.

Her memory might be a bit ropey, but between the caffeine and the sugar her brain had been pretty much put back together, and there was one image of the night before that she couldn't get from her mind.

You may now kiss the bride.

They'd all burst out laughing, finding the whole thing hilarious. But as soon as Joe's hand had brushed against her cheek, cupping her jaw to turn her face up to him, the laughs had died in her throat. He'd been looking down at her as if he were only just seeing her for the first time, as if she had been made to look different by their marriage. His lush eyelashes had swept shut as he'd leaned towards her, and she'd had just a second to catch her breath before his lips had touched hers. They had been impossibly soft, and to start with had just pressed dry and chaste against hers. She'd reached up as he had and touched his cheek, just a gentle, friendly caress of her finger against his stubbled skin. But it had seemed to snap something within him; a gasp had escaped his lips, been swallowed by hers. His mouth had parted, and heat had flared between them.

She'd closed her eyes, understood that she was giving herself up to something more powerful than the simple actions of two individuals. As her eyes had shut her mouth had opened and her body had bowed towards her husband. Her hips had met his, and instantly sparks had crackled. His hands had left her face to lock around her waist, dragging her in tight and holding her against him. His tongue had been hot and hungry in her mouth; her hands frenzied, exploring the contours of his chest, his back, his butt.

And then the applause of their audience had broken into her consciousness, and she'd remembered where they were. What they were doing.

Blood had rushed to her cheeks and she could feel them glow as she'd broken away from Joe, acknowledging the whoops with an ironic wave.

'All right, all right,' she'd said, a sip of champagne helping with the brazen nonchalance; she'd hoped that she was successfully hiding the shake in her voice. 'Hope you enjoyed the show, people.'

She'd looked up at Joe to see whether she had imagined the connection between them, whether he'd still felt it buzzing and humming and trying to pull their bodies back together. By the heated, haunted look in his eyes, she wasn't alone in this.

He was worried, and he should be, because this marriage of convenience had just got a whole lot more complicated, for both of them. It had been a laugh, a joke, until their lips had met and they had both realised, simultaneously, that the flirting and banter that had provided an edge of excitement to their dancing that night would be a dangerous force unless they got a lid on it.

In the cold light of the morning after, she knew that they needed to face the problem head-on. She broke her gaze away from him, trying to cover what they had both clearly been remembering.

'Ground rules,' she said firmly, distracting herself by taking another bite of pie. 'If we do this, there have to be ground rules to stop it getting complicated.' He nodded in agreement, and she kept talking. 'First of all, we keep this strictly business. We both need to keep our heads and be able to walk away when the time is right. Let's acknowledge that there is chemistry between us, but if we let that lead us, we're not going to be objective and make smart decisions. And I think we both agree that we need to be smart.'

'People will talk if we don't make this look good. It has to be convincing.'

'Well, duh.' She waved to the waitress for a coffee refill. 'You're really trying to teach me how to handle the press? Obviously, in public we behave as if we're so madly in love that we couldn't wait a single minute longer to get married. We sell the hell out of it and make sure that no one has a choice *but* to believe us. But that's in public. In private, we're respectful colleagues.'

He snorted. 'Colleagues? You think we can do that? You were there, weren't you, last night? You do remember?'

Did she remember the kiss? The shivers? The way that she could still feel the imprint of his mouth on hers, as if the touch of skin on skin had permanently altered the cells? Yeah, she remembered, but that wasn't what was important here.

'And that's why we need the rules, Joe. If you want to stay married to me, you'd better listen up and pay attention.'

'Oh, I'm listening, and you're very clear. In public, I'm madly in love with you. Behind closed doors I'm at arm's length. Got it. So what are your other rules?'

She resurrected the death stare. 'No cheating. Ever. If we're going to make people believe this, they have to really believe it. We can't risk the story being hijacked. Doesn't matter how discreet you think you're being, it's never enough.'

'I get it. You don't share. Goes without saying.'

She dropped her cup back onto her saucer a little heavier than she had planned, and the hot, bitter liquid slopped over the side again. 'This isn't about me, Joe. Don't pretend to know me. This is about appearances. I've already told you, this isn't personal.'

'Fine, well, if you're all done then I've got a rule of my own.'

'Go on, then.' She raised an eyebrow in anticipation.

'You move in with me.'

This time, the whole cup went over, coffee sloshing over the side of the table and onto her faded black jeans. At least she'd managed to miss her white shirt, she thought, thanking whoever was responsible for small mercies. She mopped hastily with a handful of napkins, buying her precious moments to regain her composure and think about what he had said. Of course she understood deep down that they would have to live together. But somehow, until he'd said it out loud, she hadn't believed it.

They would be alone together. *Living* alone together. No one to chaperone or keep them to their 'this is just business' word. Watching him across a diner table this morning, it wasn't exactly easy to keep her hands off him, so how were they meant to do that living alone together?

But she knew better than anyone that they had to make this look good. If her parents knew that she'd only done this to get out of the marriage to Philippe they would be so disappointed, and she didn't know that she could take doing that to them again.

Separate flats weren't going to cut it. By the time she looked back up, she knew that she seemed calm, regardless of what was going on underneath.

'Of course, that makes sense. Are you going to insist on your place rather than mine?'

'I'll need my recording studio.'

She nodded. 'Fine. So that's it, then? Three ground rules and we're just going to do this?'

'Well, if you're going to chicken out, you need to do it now.'

'I'm not eight years old, Joe. I'm not going to go through with this because you call me chicken.'

'Fine, why *are* you going to do it?' Nice use of psychology there, she thought. Act as though I've already agreed. He really did want this publicity. But it didn't matter, because she'd already made up her mind.

'I'm doing it because I don't want to hurt my family any more than I have to, and because I think it'll be good for my career.' And because it would save her from being talked into a real marriage, one which she knew she could never deserve.

'As long as you're doing it, your reasons are your own business,' Joe replied. She felt a little sting at that, like a brush of nettles against bare skin. Her own business. Damn right it was, but the way he said it, as if there really were nothing more than that between them… It didn't make sense. She didn't want it to make sense. She just knew that she didn't want it to hurt.

'So what are we going to tell people?' she asked after a long, awkward silence. 'I guess we need to get our stories straight.'

He nodded, and sipped at his coffee. 'We just keep it simple. We were swept away when we met each other yesterday, knew right away that it was love and decided we needed to be married. The guys in the band will go along with it. You don't have to worry about that.' Somehow she'd forgotten that they'd been there, egging them on, bundling them in the cab to the courthouse. When she thought back to last night, she remembered watching Joe on stage, sweat dripping from his forehead as he sang and rocked around the stage. Him grabbing her hand and pulling her to the dance floor when they'd gone on to a club after the gig, when he hadn't wanted to talk business.

She remembered the touch of his mouth on hers, as they were pronounced husband and wife.

But of course there had been witnesses, people who knew as well as she did that this was all a sham.

'What if they say something? They could go to the press.'

'They won't. Anyway, to everyone else it was just a laugh. And if anyone did say something, it'd be up to us to look so convincingly in love that no one could possibly believe them.'

'Ah, easy as that, huh.'

As they sat in the diner she realised how little thought they'd actually given this. She didn't even know when she would see him again. Her flight was booked back to London that night. She'd only been in Vegas to take this meeting. Her boss had sent her on a flying visit, instructed to try anything to get him to sign. She'd given her word that she wouldn't leave without the deal done. Would he see through them when they got back? Would he realise how far she had gone to keep to her promise?

'I'm flying home tonight,' she said.

He raised an eyebrow. 'You were pretty sure you'd get me to sign, then. Didn't think you'd have to stick around to convince me?'

'I thought you'd be on the move, actually. I was told that you were only in Vegas for one night.' She knew that the band were renowned for their work ethic and their packed tour schedule, moving from city to city and gig to gig night after night. This had been her only chance for a meeting, her boss had told her as he'd instructed her to book a flight.

If he was always on the move like that, perhaps this would be easier than she thought. It could be weeks, months, before they actually had to live together. And by then, maybe… Maybe what. Maybe things would be different? There was no point pretending to be married at all if she thought that they would have changed their minds in a few weeks. They had to stick it out longer than that. If they were going to do this, they had to do it properly.

'I am, as it happens. I'm flying back to London tonight too.'

* * *

Why had he said that? They were meant to be in the States for two more weeks. Their manager had booked them into a retreat so that he could finish writing the new album. It should have been just a case of putting the finishing touches to a few songs, but he had an uneasy feeling about it this morning. He needed to go back and look at it again. There were a few decent tracks there, he was sure. But a niggling voice in his head was telling him that he still hadn't got the big hitters. The singles that would propel the album up the streaming charts and across the radio waves. There was studio space booked for them in London in two weeks' time and it had to be fixed before then.

Their manager was going to kill him when he told him he wouldn't be showing up.

He could write in London; he had written the last album in London. It had nothing to do with Charlie. Nothing to do with her feelings, anyway. As she kept saying, this was just business. But it would look better for them to arrive home together.

Nothing to do with their feelings. Right. He would make her believe that today. Because her memory might be fuzzy but he could remember everything. Including the moment that they'd been on the dance floor, him still buzzing from the adrenaline of being on stage, her from the dancing and the music and the day and a half without sleep.

They'd moved together as the music had coursed through him, the bass vibrating his skin. She'd been trying to talk business, shouting in his ear. Contracts and terms, and commitment. But he hadn't been able to see past her. To feel anything more than the skin of her shoulder under his hand as he'd leaned in to speak in her ear. The soft slide of her hair as he'd brushed it off her face. 'Let's do this,' she'd said. 'We'd be a great team. I know that we can create something amazing together.'

She'd reached up then, making sure she had his attention—as if it would ever be anywhere but on her again. And then Ricky had said those idiotic words, the ones that no judge could take back this morning.

She'd laughed, at first, when he had proposed, assuming that he was joking. It had had nothing to do with the way she'd felt when his arm was around her. The way that that had made him feel. As if he wanted to protect her and challenge her and be challenged by her all at once.

He could never let her know how he had felt last night.

It was much better, much safer that they kept this as business. He knew what happened when you went into a relationship without any calculation. When you jumped in with your heart on the line and no defences. He wouldn't be doing it again.

And then there were the differences between them. Sure, it hadn't seemed to matter in that moment that he'd asked her to marry him, or when they were dancing and laughing and joking together, but a gig and a nightclub and beer were great levellers. When you were having to scream above the music then your accent didn't matter. But in the diner this morning there was no hiding her carefully Londonised RP that one could only acquire with decades of very expensive schooling, and learning to speak in the echoey ballrooms of city palaces and country piles.

He'd learnt that when he'd joined one of those expensive schools at the age of eleven, courtesy of his music scholarship free ride. His Bolton accent had been smoothed slightly by years away from home, first at school, and then on the road, but it would always be there. And he knew that, like the difference in their backgrounds, it would eventually come between them.

His experiences at school had made it clear that he didn't belong there.

And when he'd returned home to his parents, and their comfy semi-detached in the suburbs, he had realised that he didn't belong there any more either. He was caught between two worlds, not able to settle in either. So the last thing that he needed was to be paraded in front of the royal family, no doubt coming into contact with the Ruperts and Sebastians and Hugos from his school days.

And what about his family? Was Charlie going to come round for a Sunday roast? Make small talk with his mum with Radio 2 playing in the background? He couldn't picture it.

But he would have to, he realised. Because it didn't matter what they were doing in private. It didn't matter that he had told himself that he absolutely had to get these feelings under control, their worlds were about to collide.

It wasn't permanent. That was what he had to remind himself. It wasn't for ever. They were going to end this once a decent amount of time had passed, and in the meantime they would just have to fit into each other's lives as best they could.

Just think of the publicity. A whirlwind romance was a good story. No doubt a better one than a drunken mistake. But since when had he allowed the papers to rule on what was and wasn't a good idea for him? No, there was more to it than that. Something about waking up beside her in bed that he wasn't ready to let go of yet.

'I have an album launch party to go to first, though,' he said at last. 'What do you say to making our first appearance as husband and wife?'

CHAPTER THREE

CHARLIE ADJUSTED THE strap on her spike heels and straightened the seam of her leather leggings. As soon as the car door opened, she knew there would be a tsunami of flashes from the assembled press hordes. She was considered fair game at the best of times, and if news of the wedding had got out by now, the scrum would be worse than usual.

These shots needed to be perfect. She wasn't having her big moment hijacked by a red circle of shame.

It was funny, she thought, that neither she nor Joe had called his manager, or her boss yet, and told them about what had happened. Not the best start to a publicity campaign, which was, after all, what they had agreed this marriage was. It was more natural, this way, she thought. If there was a big announcement, it would look too fake. Much better for them to let the story grow organically.

As the limo pulled up outside the club she realised that no announcement was necessary anyway. Word had obviously got around. The hotel had arranged for them to be picked up from a discreet back door, an old habit, so she hadn't been sure whether there had been photographers waiting for her there. If there had, they'd taken a shortcut to beat them here. There were definitely more press here than a simple album launch warranted. The story was out, then.

Without thinking, she slipped her hand into Joe's, sliding her fingers between his. The sight of so many photographers still made her nervous. It didn't matter how many times she had faced them. It reminded her of those times in her childhood when she'd been pulled from the protective privacy of her family home and paraded in front of the world's press, all looking for that perfect picture of the perfect Princess. As a child she had smiled until her cheeks had ached, dressed in her prettiest pink dress, turning this way and that as her name was shouted. It had been a small price to pay, her parents had explained, to make sure that the rest of their lives were private. But as she'd got older she'd resented those days more and more, and her childish rictus grin had turned into a sullen teen grimace.

And then, when she was nineteen, and had realised that she would never be the Princess that her family and her country wanted her to be, she'd stopped smiling altogether. She remembered sitting in the doctor's office as he explained what he'd found: inflammation, scar tissue, her ovaries affected. Possible problems conceiving.

She might never have a baby, no chubby little princes or princesses to parade in front of an adoring public, and no hope of making the sort of dynastic match that would make her parents happy.

Her most important duty as a royal female was to continue her family's line. It had been drummed into her from school history lessons to formal state occasions from as far back as she could remember. Queens who had done their duty and provided little princes and princesses to continue the family line.

And things hadn't changed as much as we would all like to think, she knew. The country had liked her mother when she was a shining twenty-something. But it was when she'd given the country three beautiful royal children that they'd really fallen in love with her, when she had won their loyalty. And that was something that Charlie might never be able to do. She might never feel the delicious weight of her child in her arms. Never breathe in the smell of a new baby knowing that it was all hers.

What if she never made her parents grand-parents, and saw the pride and love in their eyes that she knew they were reserving for that occasion?

And as soon as she'd realised that, she had realised that she could never make them truly proud of her, somehow the weight of responsibility had fallen from her shoulders and she'd decided that she was never going back. If she wanted to roll out of a nightclub drunk—okay. If she wanted to disappear for three days, without letting anyone know where she was going—fine. If she wanted to skip a family event to go and listen to a new band—who cared?

Her mother insisted on a security detail, and Charlie had given up arguing that one. Her only demand was that they were invisible—she never looked for the smartly dressed man she knew must be on the row behind her on the plane, and so she never saw him. And the officers didn't report back to her mother. If she thought for a second that they would, she would have pulled the plug on the whole arrangement. That was why they'd not intervened last night: they knew she had a zero-tolerance approach to them interfering with anything that didn't affect her physical safety.

She was never going to be the perfect Princess, so why build her family's hopes up? She could let them down now, get it out of the way, in her own way, and not have to worry with blindsiding them with disappointment later.

Except it hurt to disappoint them, and it didn't seem to matter how many times that she did it. Every time, the look on their faces was as bad as the time before.

What would they say this time, she wondered, when they realised that she had married someone she had just met—so obviously to scupper the sensible match that they were trying to make for her? And she had married a rock star at that, someone who couldn't be further from the nice reliable boys that they enjoyed steering her towards at private family functions. What was the point of going along with that? she'd always thought. Entertaining the Lord Sebastians and Duc Philippes and Count Henris who were probably distant cousins, and who all—to a man—would run a mile as soon as they found out that they might not be needing that place at Eton or Charterhouse, or wherever they'd put their future son's name down for school before they had even bagged the ultimate trophy wife.

Joe leaned past her to look out of the window, and then gave her a pointed look. 'I guess our happy news is out.'

'Looks that way,' she said, with a hesitant smile. 'Ready to face the hordes?'

'As I'll ever be.' He looked confident, though, and relaxed. As if he'd been born to a life in front of the cameras, whereas she, who had attended her first photo call at a little under a day old, still came out in a sweat at the sight of a paparazzo.

But she stuck on what she'd come to think of as her Princess Scowl, in the style of a London supermodel, and pressed her knees and ankles together. It was second nature, after so many hours of etiquette lessons. Even in skintight leather, where there was no chance of an accidental underwear flash. She ran a hand through her hair, messing up the backcombed waves and dragging it over to one side in her trademark style. A glance in the rear-view mirror told her that her red lip stain was still good to go, managing to look just bitten and just kissed. She took a deep breath and reached for the door handle.

Joe stopped her with the touch of his fingertips on her knee. 'Wait.'

It was as if the leather melted away and those fingertips were burning straight into her skin. Wait? For ever, if she had to.

But before she could say, or do, anything, they were gone, as was Joe. Out of the door and into the bear pit. Then her door was wrenched open and his hand was there, waiting to pull her out into the bright desert sunshine. She gripped his hand as he helped her from the car, and the flashbulbs were going off before she was even on her feet.

Shouts reached her from every direction.

'When was the wedding?'

'Was Elvis there?'

'Were you drunk?'

And then there it was, the question that she'd never anticipated but that she realised now had been inevitable from the first.

'Are you pregnant?'

She stumbled, and it was only Joe's arm clamping round her waist and pulling her tight that stopped her falling on her face in front of the world's press. And then she was falling anyway, because Joe's lips were on hers, and her heart was racing and her legs were jelly and her lips…her lips were on fire. One of his hands had bunched in her hair, and she realised that this, this look, this feeling, was what she'd been cultivating in front of the mirror for more years than she cared to think about. Just been kissed, just been ravished. Just had Joe's tongue in her mouth and hands on her body. Just had images of hot and sweaty and naked racing through her mind. He broke away and gave her a conspiratorial smile. She bit her lip, her mouth still just an inch from his, wondering how she was meant to resist going back for more.

And then the shouts broke back into her consciousness. 'Go on—one more, Charlie!'

And the spell was broken. She wasn't going to give them what they wanted. She turned to them, scowl back in place, though there was a glow now in the middle of her chest, something that they couldn't see, something that they couldn't try and own, to sell for profit.

She grabbed Joe's hand and pulled him towards the door of the venue, ignoring the shouts from the photographers.

She dragged him through the door and into a quiet corner.

'So I guess we survived our first photo call.'

She had hoped the relative seclusion of this dark corner would give her a chance to settle her nerves, for her heartbeat to slow and her hands to stop shaking. But as Joe took another step closer to her and blocked everything else from her vision, she felt anything but relaxed.

'Are you okay? You look kind of flushed,' he asked.

'I'm fine. I just hate…never mind.' Her voice dropped away as her gaze fixed on his lips and she couldn't break it away. This wasn't the time to think about what she hated, not when she was so fixed on what she loved, what she couldn't get enough of. Like the feeling of his lips on hers.

'Joe, I thought I saw you come in. And the new missus!'

Ricky, the drummer from Joe's band, Charlie recognised with a jolt.

More flashbacks of the night before: the band laughing with them in the taxi cab to the courthouse, joking about how they were going to have to sign with her now she'd done this. She had to convince them that they'd been mistaken last night. That she'd married Joe for love at first sight, before they started talking to journalists. If it wasn't already too late.

She reached for Joe's hand and gripped it tightly in hers, hoping that it communicated everything that she needed it to.

'Hi, Ricky,' she said, plastering on a smile that she hoped broadcast newly wedded bliss and contentment.

'So your first day as husband and wife, eh. How's it working out for you?'

She tried to read into his smile what he was really saying. If only she could fake a blush, or a morning-after glow. But in the absence of that, she'd have to go on the offensive.

'Pretty bloody amazingly, actually,' she said, leaning into Joe and hoping that he'd run with this, with her.

'Really?'

Ricky gave Joe a pointed look, and it told Charlie everything that she needed to know. He had thought last night that this was all a publicity stunt, and nothing that he had seen yet had changed his mind.

'Well, I'm just glad that you both decided to take one for the team.' He grinned. 'It was a brilliant idea. I wish I'd thought of it first.'

She opened her mouth to speak, but Joe got there first.

'I'm not sure what you mean, Ricky. We're not doing this for the team. I admit it was a bit hasty, but we really meant it last night. We wanted to get married.'

'Because you're both so madly in love?'

She felt Joe's hand twitch in hers and tried not to read too much into it.

'Because it was the only thing we *could* do,' he said. 'I don't care what we call it. Love at first sight. Or lust. Whatever. I just knew that once I had Charlie in my arms there was no way I was going to let her go. And if that meant marriage, then that's what I wanted.'

Bloody hell, maybe he should have been an actor rather than a singer. He certainly gave that little speech more than a little authenticity. She leaned into him again, and this time he dropped her hand and wrapped his arm around her shoulders. She looked up at him, and there was something about the expression in his face that forced her up onto her tiptoes to kiss him gently on the lips.

‘Wow, okay,’ Ricky said as she broke away. ‘I guess I missed something last night. So, someone wants to chat with us about the new album, if you’ve got a minute.’

‘Okay,’ Joe replied, ‘but you do remember what we decided last night. We’re going to say yes to Charlie’s label. I’m not going back on my word.’

‘A bit early in the marriage for those sorts of ructions, is it?’ Ricky looked at them carefully, and Charlie knew that they hadn’t dispelled all of his doubts, regardless of how good an actor Joe was. ‘Either way, we still need to speak to them. Until this deal is signed, we schmooze everyone, as far as I’m concerned. I know the others feel the same.’

She *had* to call her boss. She couldn’t think why she hadn’t done it before now. She’d do it on the way to the plane. She glanced at her watch. They couldn’t stay long if they were going to make the flight. For a second she thought wistfully of her family’s private plane, and how much easier life had been when she’d been happy to go along with that lifestyle, to take what she didn’t feel she had earned. But it had got to the point where she simply couldn’t do it any more. If she was never going to be able to pay her parents back with the one thing that everyone wanted from her, she couldn't use their money or their privilege any more.

She had some money left to her by her grandparents—despite her protestations, the lawyers had told her that it belonged to her and there was nothing that she could do about it—and her salary from the record label.

'I'm sorry, do you mind if I talk to them?' Joe asked, turning to her.

'Of course not.' She forced a smile, trying to live in the moment and forget all of the very good reasons she should be freaking out right now. 'Go on.'

But Joe turned to Ricky. 'You go ahead,' he said. 'I'll be there in a second.'

'You all right?' he asked, when they were alone. 'Still happy with everything? Because if you're going to change your mind, now's the time…'

She drew away from him and folded her arms. 'Why would I have changed my mind?'

She didn't understand what had happened to cause this change in mood. His shoulders were tense, she could see that.

Was it because he'd just reminded Ricky of their deal to sign with her the night before? The thought made her feel slightly sick, reminded her that whatever they might say to his band, whatever story they might spin for the papers, when it came down to it, this really *was* just a publicity stunt, or a business arrangement or… whatever. Whatever it was, she knew what it wasn't. It hadn't been love at first sight. It wasn't a grand romance. It wasn't a fairy tale, and there was going to be no happy ending for her. Well, fine, it wasn't like she deserved one anyway.

But now that they were married, they had to make it work. They had to appear to be intoxicated with one another. Luckily, intoxicated was one of her fortes. She forced herself to unfold her arms and smile. 'Of course I'm all right.'

Taking a deep breath, she stepped towards him, and with a questioning look in her eye snaked her arms around those tense shoulders. She placed another chaste peck on his lips, and smiled as she drew away. 'See? Picture perfect. Everything's as we agreed. Let's go say hi to everyone.'

Under the pressure of her arms, she felt his shoulders relax and his face melted into a smile. 'Well, we could give them something to talk about first.'

His arms wrapped around her waist, and she was reminded of the rush of adrenaline and hormones that she had felt outside when he had kissed her in front of the cameras. Her breath caught as her body softened into his hold. This time when his lips met hers, there was nothing chaste about it. Her arms tightened around him as he lifted her just ever so slightly, rubbing her hips against his as she slid up his body. His arms wrapped her completely, so that her ribs were bracketed with muscular forearms, and his hands met the indents of her waist. She was surrounded by him. Overwhelmed by the dominance of his body over hers.

His mouth dominated her too, demanding everything that she could give, and it was only with the touch of his tongue that she remembered where they were. She pushed both hands on his chest, forcing him to give her space, to unwind his arms from around her waist.

She smiled as she looked at him, both of them still dazed from the effect of the kiss. 'Do you think they bought it?' she asked, remembering that just a few moments ago they had been discussing the fact that this relationship was just a business deal—that the purpose of the kiss had been to keep up appearances. But

Joe's face fell, and she knew that she had said the wrong thing.

'I think they bought it fine,' he said. 'It was a winning performance.'

Through the bite of his teeth, she knew that it wasn't a compliment.

She shook her head, then reached up and pecked him one last time on the cheek. 'Whatever it was, it blew my mind.' She met his eyes, and she knew that he saw that she was genuine. Whatever else might be going on, there was no denying the chemistry between them. It would be stupid to even try.

But beyond that, beyond the crazy hormones that made her body ache to be near his, was there something else too? A reason that the disappointment in his eyes made some part of her body hurt? She slipped her fingers between his and they walked over to where Ricky was holding court with a woman that she recognised from another record label, her competition, and a music journalist.

'So here's the happy couple,' the hack said with a smile, raising her glass to toast them. Charlie spotted a waiter passing with a tray of champagne and grabbed a flute for herself and one for Joe. She saw off half the glass with her first sip, until she felt she could stare down the journalist with impunity.

She watched Joe as they chatted, her hand trapped within his, and tried not to think about whether the warm glow of possessiveness she felt was because she'd bagged him as an artist, or a husband.

As they walked through Arrivals at Heathrow Airport, Joe felt suddenly hesitant at the thought of taking Charlie back to his apartment, definitely not something he was used to. It wasn't as if he were a stranger to taking girls home. Though in fairness home was more usually a hotel room or their place. But now that he and Charlie were back on British soil, he realised how little they'd talked about how this was going to work.

'So we said we'd stay at my place,' he reminded her as they headed towards the end of another endlessly long corridor.

'We did,' she agreed, and he looked at her closely, trying to see if there was more he could glean from these two words. But he had forgotten that his new wife was a pro at hiding her feelings—she'd had a lifetime of practice. Charlie offered nothing else, so he pushed, wanting the matter settled before they had to face the press, who were no doubt waiting for them again at the exit of the airport. Airport security did what they could to push them back, but couldn't keep them away completely. Not that he should want that, he reminded himself. They wanted the publicity. It was good for the band. It was the whole reason they were still married.

But even good publicity wasn't as important as finishing a new album would be—that thought hadn't been far from his mind the last few days. He couldn't understand how he had thought that it was nearly finished. He'd played the demo tracks over and over on the plane, and somehow the songs that he'd fine-tuned and polished so carefully no longer worked when he listened to them. They didn't make him *feel*. They had a veneer of artifice that seemed to get worse, rather than better, the more that he heard them.

His first album had come from the heart. He shuddered inwardly at the cliché. It was years' worth of pent-up emotion and truths not said, filtered through his guitar and piano. It was honest. It was him. This latest attempt… It was okay. A half-dozen of the tracks he would happily listen to in the background of a bar. But it was clean and safe and careful, and lacking the winners. The grandstanding, show-stopping singles that took an album from good to legendary.

He was still writing. Still trying. But he was out of material and out of inspiration. His adolescent experiences, his adult life of running from them had fed his imagination and his muse for one bestselling album. But he couldn't mine the same stuff for a second. It needed something new. So what was he meant to write about—how ten years on the road made relationships impossible? How his parents kept up with his news by reading whatever the tabloids had made up that week? That his only good friends had spent most of that time trapped with him in some mode of transport or another for the last decade? It was hardly rousing stuff.

'Do you want to go back there now, then?' he asked Charlie.

How was this so difficult? Was she making it that way on purpose?

She looked down at her carry-on bag. 'This is all I have with me.'

'We can send someone for your stuff.'

'No.' She didn't want anyone riffling

through her things. Occasionally she missed the discreet staff from her childhood home in the private apartments of the palace, who had disappeared the dirty clothes from her bedroom floor before it had had a chance to become a proper teenage dive, but she loved the freedom of her home being truly private. That the leather jacket that she dropped by the door when she got home would still be right there when she was heading out the next morning.

She stopped walking and looked up at him. 'Okay, so we go back to yours tonight. Tomorrow we go to my place and pack some stuff. Does that work for you? Or I could go back to my place tonight. Sleep there, if we don't want to rush into—'

'You sleep with me.'

He couldn't explain the shot of old-fashioned possessiveness that he had felt when she suggested that they sleep apart. Except... The bed share of the previous night. That was a one-off, wasn't it? He supposed they'd find out later, when she realised that his apartment's second bedroom had been converted to a recording studio. Leaving them with one king-sized bed and one very stylish but supremely uncomfortable couch to fight over. He was many things, but chivalrous about sleeping arrangements wasn't one of them. He couldn't remember the last time that he had slept eight hours in a bed that wasn't hurtling along a motorway or through the clouds. So he could promise her a chivalrous pillow barrier if she absolutely insisted, but there was no way he was forgoing his bed. Not even for her.

'For appearances' sake,' he added to his earlier comment. 'What would it look like if we spent our first night back apart?'

CHAPTER FOUR

'WHEN ARE WE going to tell our families?' Joe asked as the driver slid the car away from the kerb, and the throng of photographers who had been waiting for them grew distant in the rear window.

He was probably just hoping to fill the awkward silence, Charlie thought, rather than trying to bait her. But the niggle of guilt that had been eating away at her turned into a full-on stab. She really should have called her parents before she had left the States, but she had just kept thinking about how disappointed they were going to be in her—again—and she couldn't bring herself to do it.

But now they had another load of morning editions of the tabloids to worry about, full of their red-carpet kisses from the night before. Or was it two nights? Losing a day to the time difference when they were in the air hadn't helped her jet lag, or her sense of dislocation from the world. Whenever it was that those kisses had taken place, somehow, she didn't think that they were going to help matters.

'When we get home,' she said, cracking open a bottle of mineral water and leaning back against the leather headrest. In theory she had just had a eleven-hour flight with nothing to do but catch up on missed sleep. And it wasn't even as if she and Joe had spent the time chatting and getting to know one another. He had pulled out noise-cancelling headphones as soon as he was on board and she'd barely heard a word from him after that.

She'd shut her eyes too, pulled on a sleep mask and tried to drift off. But sleep had been impossible. First her mind had run round in circles with recriminations and criticisms; then slowly, something else had crept in. The scent of Joe's aftershave, the drumming of his fingers on the armrest as he got into whatever he was listening to. Her body remembered how she had felt that morning waking up next to him, after her dream filled with hot, sticky caresses. Before her memory returned and she remembered the idiotic thing that they had done. When he was just a hot guy in her head and not the man she had married in a fit of self-sabotage. Lust, pure and simple.

Things were anything but simple now. Attraction could be simple. A marriage of convenience could be simple too, she supposed. She was the product of generations of them. But she and Joe had gone and mixed the two, and now they were paying the price. As Joe shifted on the seat beside her she opened her eyes and watched him for a few moments.

Their late night followed by a long, sleepless flight had left him with a shadow on his jaw that was more midnight than five o'clock. She could almost feel the scratch of it against her cheek if she shut her eyes again and concentrated. She snapped herself out of it. Too dangerous. *Far* too dangerous to be having those sorts of feelings about this man. They had made this arrangement complicated enough as it was. Attraction made it more complicated still. Acting on that attraction anywhere but in the safety of the public gaze was complete madness. No, they were just going to have to get really, really good at self-restraint. She was so looking forward to shutting her bedroom door on Joe and the rest of the world and finally being able to relax and sleep off the jet lag.

Their driver hauled their bags up the stairs to his first-floor warehouse conversion, and Charlie breathed a sigh of relief when they shut the door on him. Home and private at last, all she wanted to do was sleep.

'Do you mind if I just crash?' she asked Joe. 'Which is my room?'

He looked suddenly uncomfortable. 'About that, there's actually only one bedroom.'

Determined not to lose her cool in front of him, she forced the words to come out calmly. 'What do you mean there's only one?'

She crossed the huge open living space and stood on the threshold of Joe's bedroom, her mouth gaping at what he had just told her. He was the one who had suggested they live at his apartment. He couldn't have mentioned he didn't have a guest room?

'You can't think that I'm going to sleep with you.'

'As if, Princess. You're not that irresistible, you know.' Way to kill an ego. Not that she cared right now. All she wanted was to sleep. No, she corrected herself. She needed privacy to call her parents and let them know that she'd messed up—again. And then she needed to sleep. Probably for about three days straight.

'Look, Charlie. I'm tired, I'm grouchy. I have to go call my mum and explain why I decided to get married without her there, and then I'm sleeping. The mattress is big enough for us both to starfish without getting tangled. So you do what you like, but I'm going to bed.

He was tired? *He* was grouchy?

She stood for a moment in the doorway, and could almost feel the delicious relief of slamming it shut with her on the inside. Instead, she pulled herself up to her full five feet ten inches, turned on the spot and stalked off with a grace that her deportment coach had spent months all but beating into her.

Charlie plopped down onto the couch with significantly less grace—no way was she contorting on there to sleep—and pulled out her mobile. She dialled her mum's private number, and heard her voice after a single ring. She could picture so clearly the way the Queen would be working at her desk with her phone beside her blotter, just waiting for her to call.

'Caroline.'

So much said in just one word. She'd been worried about disapproval, disappointment. But the heartfelt, unreserved concern in her mother's voice was the killer.

'Hi, Mum.'

'Charlie, are you okay?'

She dropped her forehead into her hands and wished for the first time that she had gone to do this in person. Surely it was the least her mother deserved. But—like so many of her other mistakes—it was done now, and couldn't be undone.

'I'm fine, Mum. I'm sorry, I know I should have called earlier…' Her voice tailed off and she held her breath, waiting for forgiveness.

'I'm just glad to hear from you. Are you going to tell me what happened?'

She wanted to tell the truth. To confess and tell her that she had messed up again. Her mum would forgive her…eventually. But that wouldn't stop her being disappointed. Nothing could do that. So she steeled herself to lie, to trying to cover up just how stupid she had been this time.

'I met a guy, Mum, and I don't know what happened, but we just clicked. It was love at first sight, and we wanted to get married right away.'

The long pause told her everything she needed to know about how much her mum believed that story.

'If you've made a— I mean if you've changed your mind, Charlie, we can take care of this, you know.'

It was the air of resignation that did it—the knowledge that her mother had been anticipating yet another catastrophe that strengthened her resolve.

'It wasn't a mistake, Mum. It's what I wanted. What we both wanted.' Another long pause, followed by the inevitable.

'So when do we get to meet this young man and his family?'

Her heart kicked into a higher gear as she worried what her mother was expecting—how formal and official was this going to get?

'I was thinking family dinner this weekend. Fly in and stay Friday night—how long you stay is up to you. I've already told your brother and sister. My secretary will ring with the details.'

Charlie couldn't speak. So this was real. She was going to bring Joe to meet her family, pretend that they were crazy in love. She nodded, then realised what she was doing. 'Okay, Mum, we'll be there.' Because when your mum was the Queen it was hard to say no, even more so when you had just done something you knew must have bruised her heart, if not broken it completely.

'I can't wait, darling.' The truth she could hear in her mum's voice broke her own heart in return.

She hung up and for a second let the tears that had been threatening fall onto her cheeks. Just three. Then she drew a deep breath, wiped her eyes and set her shoulders. She had, once again, got herself into an unholy mess and—once again—she would dig herself out of it. There was one other call that she knew she had to make—to her boss, Rich. But she had just disappointed one person whose approval she actually cared about. She didn't have it in her to do the double. She'd need at least a couple of hours' sleep before she could think about that.

She scrubbed under her eyes with a finger, determined to show no signs of weakness to her new husband. This was a professional arrangement and she had no business forgetting that.

As she opened the bedroom door she squared her shoulders. For just a few more hours it was just her and Joe, before the lawyers and managers and accountants wanted to start formalising everything at work. Damned right she was going to enjoy the calm before the storm.

The door opened and she looked over to the bed. *Holy cra—*

She was never going to be able to sleep again. At least not while she was pretending to be married to this man. He hadn't been lying when he'd said that there was room for the two of them to sleep side by side. It was an enormous bed. But the man she had decided to marry had chosen to starfish across it diagonally. There was barely room for a sardine either side of him, never mind anyone else.

And space wasn't the only issue. She'd assumed no naked sleeping, but maybe this was worse. The white T-shirt he must have pulled on before climbing between the sheets hugged tight around his biceps, revealing tattoos that swirled and snaked beneath the fabric, tempting her to follow their lines up his arms. The hem of the shirt had ridden up, showcasing a strip of flawlessly tanned skin across his toned back. And, just to torture her, the sheets had been kicked down to below his tight black boxers—the stretch of the fabric leaving nothing to the imagination. For half a second she thought about sleeping on that back-breaking couch. Or even calling a cab back to her own flat. But the lure of a feather mattress topper was more than she could resist. She kicked off her jeans, noting that her black boy shorts underwear was more than a little similar to her husband's. Luckily *her* white shirt covered her butt.

She crawled onto the mattress beside Joe, trying to keep her movements contained and controlled. Waking him would open the door to a host of possibilities that she didn't want to—couldn't—contemplate right now. Lying on her side on the edge of the bed, she tried to ignore the gentle rhythm of Joe's breathing beside her. She balanced on her hip, the edge of the bed just a couple of inches in front of her. So much for a deep, relaxing sleep. There was no way that was going to happen with her frightened of hitting the floor on one side or Joe on the other. No, she had to start as she meant to go on, and there was no way she was enduring marriage to a man who thought she would perch on the edge of the bed.

She snuck out an experimental toe and aimed at the vicinity of Joe's legs. When her skin met taut, toned muscle, she wasn't prepared for the flash of warmth that came with it.

For the memory of the night that flashed back with it. Of her and Joe heading for the bed in their suite, high from champagne, the roulette wheel and the new and exciting gleam on the third fingers of their left hands.

She'd jumped back onto the mattress, the bemused bellboy still standing watching them from the doorway. As Joe had approached her, the look in his eyes like a panther stalking its prey, the bellboy had withdrawn. Her eyes had locked on Joe's, then, and her breath had caught at the intensity in his gaze. And then he had tripped on the rug and fallen towards the bed headfirst, breaking the spell. She'd collapsed back in a fit of giggles, and as her eyes had closed she had been overtaken by a yawn.

She'd fallen asleep so easily the night before. Maybe she could kick him out completely. That might be the only way she was going to get to relax enough to fall asleep. She remembered the look on his face, though, when he'd told her he wasn't giving up his bed for her. She didn't think he'd take crashing to the floor well. And, really, they had enough troubles at the moment without him being any more annoyed with her. She braced herself for the heat that she knew now would come and pushed at his leg again. Success. He shifted behind her and she shuffled back a few inches on the bed. She could hear Joe still moving, but she lay stiff and still, determined not to give up her hard-won territory.

With a great roll Joe turned over, and their safe, back-to-back stand-off was broken. His breath tickled at the back of her neck, setting off a chain reaction of goosebumps from her nape to the bottom of her spine. Maybe she had been better off on the edge of the bed, because her body was starting to hum with anticipation. Her brain—unhelpful as ever—was reminding her of how good it felt to kiss him. How her body had thrummed and softened in his arms. She reached down for the duvet and tucked it tightly around her, though she didn't really need its warmth. But with her body trapped tight beneath it she felt a little more secure. As a final defence, she shoved in her earphones and found something soothing to block out the subtle sounds of a shared bed, and shut her eyes tight.

Joe stood in the bedroom doorway, surveying the scene in front of him. A pair of black skinny jeans had been abandoned by the bed, and silver jewellery was scattered on the bedside table. Dark brown hair was strewn across the pillow and one long, lean calf had snaked out from beneath the duvet. Along with the jeans on the floor, it answered a question that he'd been tempted but too much of a gentleman to find out for himself.

His wife. He had to shake his head in wonderment of how that had happened. A simple kiss from her did things to his body that he had never experienced before. He'd woken with his arms aching to pull her close and give her a proper good morning. And she was the one woman he absolutely couldn't, shouldn't fall for. They had gone into this marriage with ground rules for a good reason. They couldn't risk their careers by giving in to some stupid chemical attraction, or, worse still, by getting emotionally involved.

He'd made the mistake before of giving his heart to someone who was only out to get what she wanted. He'd learnt his lesson, and he wouldn't be making the same mistake again. And of all the women he could have married, it had to be her, didn't it? One who would throw him back into that world of privilege and wealth.

He'd spent just about every day since he was eleven years old feeling like the outsider. And now he had gone and hitched himself to the ultimate in exclusive circles. Once he and Charlie were married, there was no way of getting away from them. But he had learned how to deal with it a long time ago. Keep his distance, keep himself apart, to prevent the sting of rejection when he tried to fit in. The same rule had to apply to Charlie. It didn't matter what she had told her parents, how real they were going to make this thing look—he couldn't let himself forget that it was all for show.

He placed a cup of coffee down among her earrings and bracelets, and from this vantage point he could see the chaos emerging from her suitcase, where more shirts were spilling from the sides.

Charlie jerked suddenly upright, knocking his arm and sending the coffee hurtling to the floor.

'Crap!'

He jumped back as the scalding liquid headed for his shins. Charlie was scrambling out of bed, and grabbed her jeans from the floor to start mopping up the coffee from the floorboards. 'What the hell?' she asked, crouching over the abandoned coffee.

'I thought I'd bring you a cup of coffee in bed, you ungrateful brat.' She sat back at the insult and crossed her arms across her chest. 'I suppose I ought to expect the spoilt little princess routine,' he continued, and they both flinched at the harsh tone in his voice. 'Sorry. Look, you wait there. I'll grab a towel.'

He retreated to the kitchen and took a deep breath, both hands braced palms-down on the worktop; then grabbed some kitchen roll and headed back to the bedroom. Charlie was crouched like a toddler, feet flat on the floor, attacking the coffee with a hand towel from the bathroom. She took a slurp from the cup as she worked, swishing the towel around ineffectually, and chasing streams of coffee along the waxed floorboards and under the bed.

'Here,' he said, taking the sopping towel from her and holding out a hand to pull her up. 'I'll finish up. You drink your coffee.'

'Thanks,' she said, relinquishing the towel with a look of relief. 'And for the coffee. Sorry, I was just a bit disorientated.'

'Forgot you picked yourself up a husband in Vegas?'

'Something like that.' She grabbed her watch from the bedside table and shook off the coffee, leaving flecks of brown on the snowy white duvet cover.

'Ugh. I've got to be at work in an hour.'

She walked over to the bathroom, and he directed his gaze pointedly away from the endlessly long legs emerging from beneath that butt-skimming shirt. He had no desire to make this arrangement any more difficult than it undoubtedly was. Keeping it strictly business was the only way that it was going to work. She eyed her suitcase uncertainly. 'I've got more jeans, but I'm all out of clean tops. Can I raid your wardrobe?'

'Go for it. I'm jumping in the shower. We'll need to leave at quarter to if we're going to walk.'

She stopped riffling through the rails in his dressing room for a second.

'We?'

'I think I'd better come talk to Rich. There's a lot to go through before we can sign anything.'

Of course she hadn't forgotten that Rich had sent her out to Vegas with a job to do. So why wasn't she exactly thrilled about the prospect of going in and seeing him this morning? Because this hadn't been what he'd meant, she knew. It hadn't been what she'd wanted either. If this was a casting-couch situation she wasn't sure which of them had been lying back and thinking of the job, but she knew that she was good at what she did. She knew that she could have bagged this signing without bringing her personal life or family into the picture. But who was going to believe that now?

Her face fell, and somehow he knew exactly what she was thinking.

'You think he's going to be pissed at you?'

'Why would he be? He sent me out there to close this deal. Job done, mission complete. He's going to be thrilled.'

'Really? So why don't you look happy about it?'

'It's nothing.'

'It's clearly something.'

He sat on the edge of the bed as she turned back to the wardrobe and started looking through his shirts again. Sliding them across the rail without paying much attention.

'I'm just not sure how he's going to react to…this.' She waved a hand between them so he understood exactly what 'this' was. His hackles rose.

'You told me you weren't involved with anyone. Are you telling me you and he are…a thing? Because that would be a major problem. I can't believe you'd—'

'It's nothing like that.' She grabbed hold of a shirt and pulled it from the hanger. 'God, why does everyone assume that any professional relationship I have is based on sex?' He lifted one eyebrow as he took in her half-dressed form and the unmade bed.

'Oh, get lost, Joe. This is nothing to do with sex. This was *your* idea. I'd have got you to sign anyway.'

'Really? Why did you say yes, then?' She had been starting off to the bathroom, but she stopped halfway across the room, his shirt screwed up and crumpled in her hand.

'Oh, why does a party girl do anything, Joe?' Her smile was all public, showing nothing of the real woman he had spent the last couple of days with. 'I'm an idiot. I was drunk. It was a laugh.' It was what everyone would assume, there was no doubt about that—but what was most shocking to him was that she didn't believe that any of those statements were true. So if it hadn't been just for a laugh, and it wasn't about her job either, then why had she done it?

He waited for the water to shut off and for Charlie to emerge from the bathroom before he grabbed his wash bag from his suitcase. She kept her back to him as she emerged and headed straight into the dressing room. Respecting her obvious need for privacy, and reluctant to continue their argument, he went straight into the bathroom and locked the door.

So what was the deal with her boss if she wasn't sleeping with him? Why was she so bothered about what he would think about their marriage? Their reasons for staying together were still good. The papers had been full of stories about the two of them, and there had been talk about the anticipation of their new album. It was exactly the sort of coverage that you couldn't buy. Her boss would be able to see that. He should be pleased that she'd got the job done and with a publicity angle to boot.

He stepped under the spray of the shower and let the water massage his shoulders. Maybe he should let her go and deal with her boss on her own. But he was keen to get this contract signed. He had meant what he had said. He'd been impressed with what the label had pitched to him—he would have signed even without Charlie turning up in Las Vegas.

He followed in her footsteps to the dressing room and wasn't sure whether to be disappointed or relieved that the towel had been discarded on the floor and she was fully dressed. One of his shirts was cinched in at the waist with a wide belt of studded black leather. A pair of black leather leggings ended in spike-heeled boots and she was currently grimacing into the mirror as she applied a feline ring of heavy black eyeliner.

'Walk of shame chic,' she said as she met his eye in the mirror. 'What do you think?'

'I think that now you're a married woman we can't call it the walk of shame. This is home. If you want it to be.' He leaned back against the wall as she paused with a tube of something shiny and gold in her hand. His eyes met hers in the mirror, and he gave a small smile. Relaxing in that moment, he enjoyed their connection—the first since they had woken up that morning. And he remembered again that feeling when he had first met her. When he had glanced across the stage and seen her in the wings, watching him. How they had danced and felt so in tune, so together, that the idea of marriage had seemed inevitable, rather than idiotic.

He laughed as she broke their eye contact to apply a coat of mascara, complete with wide open mouth.

'Come on,' he said, heading to the kitchen. 'I'll make another coffee.'

She glanced at her watch, returning his smile.

'We might have to drink on the go.'

He couldn't deny that he was startled. Princess Caroline all worried about being late for work the morning after bagging the biggest signing of her career. She was just full of surprises.

In the kitchen he set the coffee machine going and grabbed his only travel mug from a cabinet. 'Okay, but we're sharing, then,' he shouted back to her as he added frothy steamed milk.

By the door, he grabbed wallet and keys from the tray on the console where he'd dropped them the night before. Waiting for Charlie, he had an unimpeded view of her kicking her coffee-stained jeans towards her suitcase, and swiping some of the jewellery from the bedside table, but knocking the rest of it under the bed. Spot the girl who'd grown up with staff, he thought again to himself. They were going to have to talk about this at some point, he realised. He wasn't going to pick up after her like some sort of valet.

Was that how she saw him, he wondered—on a par with the staff? Barely visible in a room? She swept past him and out of the door; then drew up short in the corridor, clearly surprised that he wasn't just following in her wake.

'Are you coming?' she asked over her shoulder.

Slowly, Joe turned his key in the lock and then walked towards her. He took a long sip of coffee from the travel mug and then met her eye.

'You're not a princess here, sweetheart,' he told her gently. 'Home means you do your own fetching and carrying.'

Her brows drew together and he knew he'd pissed her off. 'I'll start by carrying this, then, shall I?' She took the coffee from him and walked into the lift, letting the door close in his face behind her.

Charlie swiped them into the office with her key card and waved at the receptionist on her way past. Avalon Records was based in a run-down old Regency villa on a once fashionable square. The grandeur of the high ceilings and sweeping staircases was in stark contrast to the workaday contents. Laminate wood desks had been packed into every corner of the building, and tattered swivel chairs fought for space with stacks of paper and laser printers.

She headed to her desk with eyes forward, intent on not letting anyone—especially Joe—see how nervous she was. Not that she needed to worry about that. She had been so keen to get into the office early that the place was practically deserted. She reached her desk and stashed her bag in a drawer, making herself busy for just a few more moments, turning on the computer and getting everything straight in her head so that the minute Rich arrived she could sell the hell out of this situation.

This was a good day, and there was no way she was leaving Rich's office until he agreed with her. Not only had she closed the deal that Rich had sent her out there to do, she had tied Joe and The Red Kites to their future in the closest way possible. Rich should—and he would—be eternally grateful. This was a massive coup for their indie label, tempting the hottest band of the year away from the big multinationals. She grabbed a couple of files and a notebook from under a pile of papers and then turned back to Joe.

He was staring at her desk with a mixture of shock and despair.

'What?' she asked, alarmed by his expression.

'Oh, my God. You're a slob.' He laughed as he spoke, his eyes wide. She leaned back against her desk and crossed her arms across her chest.

'I am so not.'

'You totally are. I thought maybe back at my place it was because we were both still living out of our cases. I need to clear you some space in the war…' His voice drifted and a shadow crossed his expression before he shook it off and got back to the point. 'But this proves it. I mean…how do you find anything?'

She waved the files in her hand at him.

'Because they're exactly where I left them.'

He shook his head again. 'But wouldn't they also be exactly where you left them if they were…say…filed neatly in a drawer?'

She raised her brows. 'You wouldn't by any chance be interfering, would you, Joe? Because this is my desk, and my office, and my job, and you don't get to boss me around here.'

He snorted out a breath. 'Oh, right, because at home you're so biddable and accommodating.' He laughed again, taking a step closer until she was trapped between him and the desk. She could smell his shower gel, the same one that she'd borrowed that morning, knowing even as she'd done it that she was going to be haunted by this reminder of him all day. She looked up at him, enjoying the novelty of a man who was still a smidge taller than her, even when she was in heels.

'I'm not interfering. I'm just getting to know you. We can talk about this more at home.' He took another half-step closer and she hitched a butt cheek onto her desk, looking for just a little more space, a little more safety. Breathing space for sensible, professional decision-making.

Then Joe lifted his hand and even without knowing where it was heading—hair, cheek, lips—she knew it would be more than her self-control could stand. She grabbed his hand mid-air, but that didn't help. It just pulled him closer as their linked hands landed on the desk by her hip. The front of his thighs pressed against hers, long and lean and matched so perfectly to her body he could have been made for her. She could feel the gentle pressure of his breath on her lips, and her eyes locked on his mouth as she remembered the times that they had pressed against hers. Her brain was desperately trying to catch up with the demands of her body. Remember the agreements they had made. They were meant to be madly in love in public. They were business associates when they were home. But what were they to each other here? In this public place, but with no one there to see them.

She dragged her gaze away for a moment, over Joe's shoulder to the still-deserted office. She had wanted to be in early. To show Rich that she was still as committed—as professional—as ever. But it had left her and Joe dangerously secluded.

His fingers untangled from hers, and she was hit with syncopated waves of regret then relief. But neither lasted long as his hand completed its original journey and landed this time on her cheek. His palm cupped her face as he tilted her head just a fraction. The sight of his tongue sneaking out to moisten his lips set off a chain reaction from the tight, hard knot low in her pelvis to the winding of her arms around his shoulders to the low sigh that escaped her throat as she closed her eyes and leaned in, waiting for the touch of his mouth.

A door slammed behind her and she jumped back, whacking her thighs against her desk in the process. She pushed at Joe's chest, knowing even before she turned to look at Rich's office what she was going to find.

Her boss was standing in front of the closed door to his office, leaning back against it with his arms crossed. Proof that the slam had been entirely for effect. Bloody drama queen, Charlie cursed him under her breath.

'The lovebirds return,' Rich said, leaning forwards and extending his arm to shake Joe's hand. 'It's good to see you again, Joe. We weren't expecting you. Are you just seeing the wife to work, or...?'

'Actually, Rich, we have good news.' Charlie watched her boss's face closely, trying to judge his reaction. 'Joe and the rest of the guys are all in agreement. They want to sign with us. Joe wanted to come and give the good news in person this morning.'

Rich's professional smile didn't give anything away, but she knew him well enough to see the slight hint of tightness around his eyes that told her that this wasn't unmitigated pleasure.

'That is great news,' he said, clapping Joe on the back. 'I guess this is a pretty good week for us all, then. Congratulations to you both. Married? Love at first sight, the papers are saying. I have to admit, I was surprised not to hear it from the horse's mouth.' He gave Charlie a pointed look and she pulled herself up to her full height, determined not to act like a chastised teenager. She had every right to do just what she wanted. She didn't need Rich's permission, or his approval, to marry whomever she chose.

'You know how it is, Rich. The papers knew what was happening almost before we did. We didn't have a chance to tell people ourselves.'

'Funny how that happens, isn't it?' Rich said with a quirk of his eyebrow. So he definitely wasn't going to buy 'love at first sight' then. Time for Plan B.

Joe looked from her to Rich, and must have picked up on the atmosphere between them.

'Look, we just wanted to give you *this* news in person,' Joe said. 'I know that there's loads to work out with the lawyers and stuff so just let me know when you want to start.' He leaned forward to shake Rich's hand again before turning back to Charlie. She waited to hear Rich go back into his office, but the click of the door handle didn't come. Was this a test? Was he trying to see if this was all for show?

She didn't have time to worry about it as Joe's lips descended on hers. His hands framed her face, his fingertips just teasing at her hairline. His lips were warm and soft as they pressed against her mouth, full of promise and desire. But then his hands dropped to her shoulders as he broke away, and when she opened her eyes she was met by a twinkling expression in his. 'See you at home, love.'

He swept out of the office with a final wave at Rich, and she fought the urge to lean back against her desk to catch her breath.

Instead her hands found the files that she'd grabbed before Rich had arrived, and she stalked into his office with her head held high.

'Are you ready to get started? We've got a lot to cover.'

Rich stood in the doorway, not joining her at the table as she pulled out a chair and sat. Then shook his head as he took in her determined glare. 'I'll be with you in a second.'

Five minutes later he returned with two cups of coffee and a look of determination that matched her own.

She was reading through a boilerplate contract, making notes in the margin with a red pen, and Rich waited for her to finish scribbling before he sat.

'Here, have a caffeinated peace offering. Have you slept at all since you left for the airport? I'm betting your body has no idea what time zone it's in right now.'

'Thanks.' She took the coffee and realised that he was right. She should be exhausted, but she wasn't. Something to do with having a brand-new husband she wasn't sure if she was meant to be keeping her hands off or not, she supposed.

'So are you going to tell me what happened?'

'I thought you said you already knew.'

'I told you I'd read the papers. I want the real story. From you, preferably. I think I deserve that. This affects us all. This is work. When I sent you out there to seal the deal, I didn't mean do *any*thing. I thought maybe...I don't know. The Princess thing: sometimes it works. I never expected you to... Just... What happened, Charlie?'

She looked him in the eye, still trying to work out her angle. How much she should share. How much she should hide. But Rich was right. This went beyond her personal life. She and Joe had made a calculated business decision—he couldn't expect her to keep it from the head of the business.

'We got carried away. Vegas, you know.' She gestured vaguely with her hands. 'We'd had too much to drink. We thought it would be funny. And that, you know, the publicity wouldn't be a bad thing for the band.'

'So it wasn't…' He hesitated, and Charlie just knew he was trying to find the right words. The ones that would annoy her the least. She prayed he wasn't about to ask the question she knew deep down was coming. 'It wasn't a quid pro quo deal. Nothing to do with the contract.'

She bristled, even though she'd been expecting it.

'What are you implying, Rich? Because if you think that I would do that—that I would need to… There's nothing I can say to that.'

Rich held out his hands for peace.

'I'm just trying to understand here, Charlie. I wasn't implying anything. So you thought it was a laugh, to celebrate the deal, and the publicity wouldn't exactly harm the band. But… now? What's going on now? You're living together?'

'We thought it would look better if it was love at first sight rather than a Vegas mistake. We're both committed to keeping up the pretence until the publicity won't be as harmful.'

'And it's all for show?' Rich asked. She nodded. 'So that little moment I walked in on earlier?'

'All part of the act.'

Rich sighed, non-committal. 'Okay, all of that aside, this is an amazing opportunity for us. Great job on getting the signing. I knew that I could trust you to take care of it.'

Charlie straightened the papers in front of her, enjoying the warm glow of Rich's praise for her work. She'd survived the first meeting: it could only get better from here.

'So how did it go with your boss after I left?' Joe asked when she arrived home that evening. 'It looked like things were about to get heated between you.'

She crossed to the fridge and surveyed the contents as she thought about it.

'It was a bit hairy at first,' she admitted as

she grabbed a couple of beers and waved one in Joe's direction. He took them both from her and reached behind him into a drawer to find a bottle opener.

'Does he always get so involved in his staff's personal lives?'

'Only when they go around marrying potential clients.'

He raised his eyebrows in a 'fair enough' expression, pulling out the bar stool next to him at the kitchen island.

'Why do you care so much what he thinks anyway? If you're so adamant that there's nothing going on between you.'

'Jealous again, darling?' She threw him some serious shade while taking a sip of her beer and resting her hip on the stool. The hardness of his gaze drew her up short. 'Don't be an idiot, Joe. I'm not impressed or in the least turned on by the jealousy thing. Drop it.'

'Okay,' he conceded. 'So there's nothing romantic going on between you. Tell me what that weird vibe was, then. Why were you afraid of disappointing him?'

'He's my boss. I'd quite like to not get fired. Are you so much of a celeb these days that you don't remember what it's like to hold down a job?'

'Said the Princess.'

'You wanted to know why I don't want to disappoint Rich? Because he's the only one who doesn't call me Princess. Even when others aren't doing it to my face, they still treat me differently, and it drives me crazy. Rich is the only person who doesn't make exceptions or allowances. He's the one person who treats me like a normal goddamn human being and expects me to act like one. If I stepped out of line he'd fire me in a heartbeat.'

'And you'd walk straight into another job.'

She resisted the urge to throw her beer at him. 'Maybe I would. But not one that I deserve. Not one that I could do as well as the one I have now. Rich has made me work my arse off for every achievement. Every signing. Every bloody paycheque has been in exchange for my blood, sweat and tears. He's the only one who could see that I can do it. I work hard, I earn my keep. When I let him down, I'm proving them right. All the people who just expect the world to fall into my lap.'

Which was why there was no way that she was walking away from the life that she'd built for herself, just because she'd promised her parents she'd come home at some fixed point in time.

'I'm sorry, I didn't mean to.'

'It's a sore point, okay. Because I have let him down. This whole thing is stupid. It's beneath me. I messed up, and I don't like having it pointed out to me by the people whose opinion I value.'

He gave her a long, assessing look. 'We never talked about how it went with your parents, did we?'

She knocked back another long glug of beer.

'They want to meet you.'

'Mine too.'

She caught his eye, and managed a tentative smile. 'How do you reckon that's going to go?'

'My mum asked if she needed to wear a hat.'

Frothy beer hit her nose as she snorted with laughter.

'What did you tell her?'

'That I had no idea. I have no idea how this works.' The laughter died in his eyes and he looked suddenly solemn.

'Are you freaked out by it? The royalty thing? Because I thought you went to Northbridge School. My cousins are there. And you didn't seem all that impressed when I arrived in Vegas.'

He hesitated; the last thing that he wanted was to talk about his school days. He'd been awkward enough there, the scholarship kid from up north. And that was before the school's very own Princess—she didn't need the royal blood to call herself that—had used and humiliated him. 'Yeah, I knew your cousins at school,' Joe said, 'but we weren't friends. I didn't exactly click with my classmates.'

'School can be a cruel place.'

'I guess.' He took another swig of his beer and thought back. It had been a long time since he'd really thought about that part of his life. After he'd been ignominiously dumped in front of half his school year, he'd taken the lesson, moved on, and tried to forget about the humiliation. 'There wasn't any bullying or anything like that. The masters would never have stood for it. It's just, I didn't fit in, you know.' There was no need to tell her the whole ugly story. It had been embarrassing enough the first time around.

'And you're worried it's going to be like that

with my family?' Charlie leaned forward and rested her elbow on the bar and her chin on her hand as she asked the question. 'They're really nice, you know,' she said earnestly. 'Well, my brother's an idiot, but every family has one of those.'

'I'm sure they are nice, Charlie. But they're different. We're different. And that's not something that we can change.' The last time that he'd been around people who moved in royal circles, the fact that he was different had become a currency in a market that he hadn't understood. Luckily, he was older and wiser now. He knew to look out for what people wanted from him, and to make sure he was getting a good deal out of it too. He also knew that no one was ever going to see their match as a marriage of equals.

'It's a good job that this is just all for show, then,' she added. 'So my family won't be making you uncomfortable for long.'

A look of pain flashed across her face, and he wondered what had caused it. It was too deep, too old to have been caused by this argument.

'It doesn't matter,' she said after a long pause, turning away from him almost imperceptibly. 'I'm never going to marry, so you don't have to worry about some future husband being trapped in that world.'

'I hate to break it to you, but it's a bit late for never.' He leaned in closer, nudging the footrest of her stool, trying to bridge the gulf that had suddenly appeared between them.

'Well, except this isn't real, is it?' she said.

He nodded, trying to hide his wince at the unexpected pain her statement had caused. Time for a change of subject, he thought. 'So why are you never getting married? Well, getting married again.'

'It's just not for me.' She shuffled to the back of her stool, reinstating the distance that he had tried to breach.

'Wow. That's enlightening.' She was hiding something from him, he knew it. Something big. And while she could keep her secrets if she wanted—it worried him. Because how was he meant to know how to handle this situation if he didn't have all the information? With all the women that had come before her, he knew exactly what they wanted, and they knew what he wanted in return.

With Charlie, despite their best efforts to keep this businesslike, he knew that everything she said carried shades of meaning that he didn't understand. It made him nervous, knowing that he was making calculations without all of the information he needed.

'Look, what does it matter, Joe? I wouldn't make a good wife, it wouldn't be fair for me to get married—not to someone who actually wanted to be my husband. But you'll have a chance to see them all for yourself. When I spoke to my mother yesterday she invited us over for dinner with the family on Friday. We'll need to stay. It's too far to fly there and back in an evening.'

'Yeah, great,' he said, though he knew that his lack of enthusiasm was more than clear.

'Anyway, I don't want to talk about this any more. How about we go out? I'm not sure what's going on with the jet lag, but I'm not sleeping any time soon. We could go get a drink—I know a place not far from here.'

'Like a date?' he asked, uncertainly. Had she suddenly decided that that was what she wanted?

'Like a chance for the press to see us as loved-up and glowing newly-weds.'

He nodded, trying to work out whether he was relieved or disappointed that it was all part of the act. 'Wouldn't newly-weds be more interested in staying home and getting to know one another?'

She spoke under her breath so quietly he could barely hear her reply: 'All the more reason to go out.'

CHAPTER FIVE

SHE PULLED THE front door closed behind them while she smudged on a bright red lip crayon. The bar was a ten-minute walk away. She'd been to their open mic night a few times, looking out for artists that she'd seen online but wanted to check out playing live before she decided if she was interested. As they turned the corner by the bar, though, she realised that this wasn't going to be one of those nights where she struck professional gold. And when they walked in and saw the screens showing lyrics, her worst fears were confirmed. It was no-holds-barred, no-talent-required, hen-parties-welcome karaoke. A trio of drunk students were belting out a rock classic, spilling pints of beer with their enthusiasm. Well, at least their taste in music couldn't be faulted, Charlie thought, boosting the roots of her hair with her fingers in honour of her spirit sister.

'Well, they're certainly going for it,' Joe said with a grin that slipped slightly as they hit a particularly painful note. 'This your usual kind of place?'

She looked around. The place itself was great: a shiny polished wood bar, real-ale pumps gleaming and—importantly—well stocked with decent beer. Plus there was plenty of gin on the shelves, and good vodka on ice for later in the evening. But most importantly of all, the manager, Ruby, had her number and would call with any hot tips for new acts she might be interested in.

'Charlie!' Ruby greeted her with a smile. 'Don't usually see you here on a Tuesday. Don't tell me this is your honeymoon. That would be too tragic.'

Charlie forced a laugh at this reminder of her newly married status.

'I wish. No time for a honeymoon. But Joe—or we, now, I guess—live just round the corner and we fancied a quiet drink. I'd say you'd be seeing more of me, but…' She looked over at the singing students.

'Wanted to try something new. Don't worry, I won't be repeating the experiment.'

They all watched the tone-deaf trio with similar expressions of amusement.

'Sorry,' Charlie added, realising that she hadn't introduced Joe. 'Joe, this is Ruby, she runs this place. Ruby, this is Joe, my…er…'

'Her husband,' Joe filled in, sliding one arm around her waist and with the other leaning over the bar to shake Ruby's hand.

'I read about your news. Congrats! Vegas, huh. You guys have a wild time?'

'"Wild" is one word for it.'

'The best.'

Charlie, remembering her part, relaxed into Joe's arms. Ruby was watching them carefully, and Charlie wondered what she was thinking. Was she trying to judge whether they were for real? Were they going to face this scrutiny from everyone they met? She might not count Ruby as quite a friend, but Charlie would normally have at least considered her an ally. Well, they would just have to convince her, she decided. Because they were going to make this pretence of a marriage work. The alternative was to disappoint her family even more than she already had.

She just had to remember that it was all make-believe. She didn't get to be the glowing newly-wed in real life. Being a wife, like being a princess, came with certain responsibilities, certain expectations that she knew she couldn't fill. There was no point letting herself fall for a guy only to have him up and leave when he found out that she might not be a complete woman.

Charlie ordered a couple of beers and led Joe over to one of the booths in the back of the bar. It was comfy and private, upholstered in a deep red leather, and just the sort of spot that a loved-up couple would choose, she thought.

'They're really going for it, huh,' Joe said, indicating the girls on the karaoke, who had moved on from rock to an operatic power ballad. He took a swig of the ale, and Charlie watched as his throat moved. His head was thrown back, so he couldn't see her watching him. From inside the sleeve of his tight white T-shirt she could see half a tattoo, weaving and winding around his arm. She was concentrating so hard on trying to trace the pattern that she didn't notice at first that his eyes had dropped and she'd been totally busted.

'Looking at something you like?' It could have sounded cheesy. It *should* have sounded cheesy. But somehow the sincerity in his gaze saved it. 'You wanna see the rest of it?'

Okay, so that was definitely flirtatious. She looked around quickly to see if anyone was eavesdropping. Surely if they were already hitched she should know what his tats looked like.

Ruby was serving at the bar, the drunk girls were still singing enthusiastically, and most of the other customers had been scared off.

She slipped off her bench and darted round the table, sliding in beside Joe until her thigh was pressed against his.

'All yours,' he said, lifting his arm. Her fingertips brushed at the edge of the cotton T-shirt, which was warm and soft from contact with his skin. She traced the band that wound around his bicep, looking up and meeting his eye when he flinched away from her touch as she reached the sensitive skin near his underarm.

'Ticklish?'

'Maybe.' One side of his mouth quirked up in a half-smile, and she filed that information away, just in case she should ever need it.

She shouldn't ever need it, she reminded herself.

This was just an arrangement, and she had no business forgetting it. No business exploring his body, even something as seemingly innocent as an arm. Her body remembered being in bed with him. It remembered those kisses. The way that she had arched into him, desperate to be closer. She shot off the bench, diving for safety on the other side of the table.

'It's nice. I like it.' She tried to keep her voice level, to prevent it giving away how hard she was finding it to be indifferent to him.

'Well, there's plenty more. But maybe we should keep those under wraps for now.' She nodded. Not trusting herself to reply to that statement. She took a sip of beer, hoping the chilled amber liquid would cool her blazing face.

'So the open mic here's usually good?' Joe asked, and she jumped on the change of subject gratefully.

'It is,' she said. 'Very different from tonight. It's normally pretty professional. I've found a couple of great artists here.'

'You like to find them when they're still raw?'

'Of course. I mean a fully formed band with a track record is pretty great too.' She inclined her head towards him and he smiled. 'But there's something about finding raw talent and helping it to develop. It's… It's what gets me to work on a Monday morning when sometimes I'd rather drag the duvet over my head.'

'Must be tough to stay motivated when you don't really have to work.'

She dropped her bottle on the table a little harder than was strictly necessary. 'And why do you think I don't have to work?'

'Oh, I don't know, royal families are all taxpayer-funded, right?'

She placed both palms face down on the table, forcing herself to appear calm, not to slam them in a temper. 'The *working* royals are taxpayer-funded. Yes. And the key word there is "working". Do you know what the royal family is worth to my country's economy in terms of tourism alone? Not that it matters, because I opted out. I don't do official engagements and I don't take a penny.'

'Come on, though. You've never had to struggle.'

'Oh, because a wealthy family solves all problems. We all know that.'

She wished it were true. She had asked the doctor when she had first got her diagnosis whether there was anything that could be done, and the answer was a very equivocal 'maybe'.

Maybe if she threw enough money at the problem, there might be something they could do to give her a chance of conceiving. But it wouldn't take just money. It would take money and time and invasive procedures. Fertility drugs in the fridge and needles in her thighs. It could mean every chance of the world discovering she was a failure on the most basic level, and absolutely no guarantee that it would even work. No, it was simpler to accept now that marriage and a family weren't on the cards for her and move on.

'Where did you pick up this chip on your shoulder, anyway?' Charlie asked. 'I thought your education was every bit as expensive as mine.'

He looked her in the eye, and for a moment she could see vulnerability behind his rock-star cool.

'I had a full scholarship,' he said with a shrug.

'Impressive.' Charlie sat back against the padding of the bench. 'Northbridge don't just hand those out like sweeties. Was it for music?'

She was offended by his expression of surprise. What, did he expect her to recoil at the thought that he didn't pay his own school fees? God, he really did think that she was a snob. Well, it was high time she straightened that one out. Finishing her beer in one long gulp, she slid out of the booth and held out her hand to pull Joe up.

'Somehow,' she said, when he hesitated to follow her, 'you seem to have got totally the wrong idea about what sort of princess I am. We're going to fix that. Now.'

His expression still showing his reluctance, he allowed her to pull him to standing, but leaned back against the table, arms folded over his chest.

'How exactly do you plan to do that?'

'We, darling husband, are going to sing.'

He eyed the karaoke screens with trepidation.

'Here?'

'Where else?' But he still didn't look convinced.

'Are you any good?'

'I'm no music scholar, but I hold my own. Now, are you going to choose something or am I?'

She grabbed the tablet with song choices

from Ruby at the bar, who looked eternally grateful that someone would be breaking the students' residency.

'Are you going to help choose? Because I'm strongly considering something from the musical theatre oeuvre.'

That cracked his serious expression and he grinned, grabbing the back pocket of her jeans and pulling her back against the table with him, so they could look at the tablet side by side.

'As if you'd choose something that wasn't achingly cool.'

She swiped through the pages in demonstration.

'Hate to break it to you, but there's a distinct lack of "achingly cool". The only answer is to go as far as possible in the other direction. We go for maximum cheese.'

'I was so afraid you were going to say that.'

'Come on.' She swiped through another couple of choices until she landed on a classic pop duet. 'It's got to be this one.' She hit the button that cued up the song and bought another round at the bar to tempt the drunk girls away from their microphones. With another couple of beers for her and Joe in hand, she stepped up onto the little stage.

She glanced around the bar—the girls had done a good job of emptying the place, but a few tables had stuck it out, like her and Joe, and now had all eyes on her. She could see the cogs whirring as they tried to place her face. Obviously not expecting to see a princess at the karaoke night. Even one with her reputation.

'It's a duet!' she shouted to him from the stage. 'Don't you dare leave me hanging!'

She held out her hand to him again and this time he grabbed it enthusiastically, pulled himself up to the stage beside her and planted a heavy kiss on her lips.

The surprise of it stole her reason for a moment, as her breath stopped and her world was reduced to the sensation of him on her. She lifted her hands to his arms, bracing herself against him, feeling unsteady on the little stage as one arm slid around her waist and his hand pressed firmly on the small of her back, pulling her in close.

Her fingers teased up his bicep; though her eyes were closed, her fingers traced the pattern of his tattoo from memory, nudging at the hem of his sleeve as they had earlier, keen to continue their exploration.

A wolf whistle from the crowd broke into their little reverie, and Charlie looked up, only to be greeted with the cameras of several phones pointing in her direction. Well, they'd be in the papers again. She shrugged mentally and reminded herself that that was the whole idea of this marriage.

That was why he'd kissed her.

It took a few moments for reality to break through. For her to remember that of course he'd only kissed her because they had an audience. This wasn't real—they just had to make it look that way. And just as her confidence wavered, and she wondered why that thought hurt so much, the music kicked in and Joe passed her a microphone.

'Come on then, love. Show me what you've got.'

She pulled her hair to one side, puckered up her finest pout and prepared to rock out.

They made it through the first verse without making eye contact, never mind anything more physical, but as they reached the chorus Joe reached around her waist and pulled her back, so her body was pressed against him from spike earrings to spike heels. She faltered on the lyrics, barely able to remember how to breathe, never mind sing.

She looked round at Joe to see if it had had the same effect on him, but when she saw his face she knew that he wasn't feeling what she was feeling. He was just feeling the music: every note of it. His throaty, husky voice giving the pop song a cool credibility it had ncver had before.

She pulled away to see him better, and though she picked up the words and joined in, it was only a token effort. Backing vocals to his masterful performance. This was why she'd agreed to marry him. The man Joe became on stage was impossible to refuse. She had kicked herself every minute since she'd woken up with a Vegas husband she no longer wanted, asking how she could have been so stupid.

But she hadn't been stupid, she realised now. It was just that they had been so magnetically drawn to one another because of his passion for music—any music—that it would have been pointless even trying to resist. Joe's eyes opened as the song slowed, and their gazes met, freezing them in the moment.

Does he feel it too? she wondered. Or had he just been so high on the adrenaline of performance that he would have agreed to marry anyone who had crossed his path?

She could see his adrenaline kicking up a notch now. His gestures growing more expansive, his grin wider, his eyes wilder.

She sang along, trying to keep pace with his enthusiasm, but whatever performance gene he'd been born with, she was clearly lacking.

The song finished with an air-guitar solo from Joe, and a roar of applause from the bar. She'd been so intent on watching him that she hadn't noticed the place fill up. From the many smartphones still clutched in hands, she guessed that they were about to go viral.

Joe grabbed her around the waist, and before she could stop him, before she could even think about whether she wanted to, his mouth was on hers, burning into her body, her mind, her soul, with his intensity. His hands were everywhere: on her butt, in her hair, gently traipsing up her upper arm. His lips were insistent against hers, demanding that she gave herself to him with equal passion. And his tongue caressed hers with such intimacy that it nearly broke her. Soft and hard, gentle and rough, he surprised her with every touch.

When, finally, he pulled away, they both

gasped for air, and she was grateful his arms were still clamped around her waist, keeping her upright. And that she'd turned so that her back was to the bar, so no one would be able to see her flaming red cheeks or the confusion in her eyes.

'Uh-oh. Looks like we've got an audience,' Joe said, and Charlie registered that the surprise in his voice seemed genuine. Had he really not noticed that they were being watched? Because if not, that kiss needed an explanation. The knowledge that it was all for show had been the only thing keeping her from losing her mind. He couldn't go and change the rules now.

'Are you up for another?' Joe asked.

Another song? Another drink? Another kiss? None of the options seemed particularly safe after that performance.

'I think my singing days are done,' she said with a smile, jumping down from the stage and heading back to the relative safety of their booth.

'Where did they all come from?' Joe asked, drinking the beer he'd abandoned when he'd gone into performance mode.

'Happened quickly, huh.'

'So fast I didn't even notice.'

Then why did you kiss me? The question hung, loud and unspoken, in the air.

'So what's your family like?' Charlie asked, suddenly desperate for a change of subject. 'You're from up north, right?'

Joe nodded, and named a town near Manchester. Of course she already knew where he'd grown up from her research into the band, but small talk seemed the safest option open to them at the moment. 'They must have been proud of you. For the scholarship. For everything since.'

'Of course. They were chuffed when I got into the school. It was their idea, actually. My mum was a gifted pianist but never had the opportunity for a career in music. They wanted me to have the best.'

'Sounds like a lot of pressure.' If there was one thing she understood it was the heavy weight of family expectation. But Joe shrugged, non-committal.

'Their motives were good. Still are.'

'But you weren't happy?'

'It was an amazing opportunity.'

'That's not what I asked.'

He sighed and held up his palms. 'I don't

like to sound ungrateful. I have no reason to complain. The school funded me. My parents made sacrifices.'

'You remember who you're talking to, right? I do understand that having the best of everything doesn't always make you happy. It doesn't make you a bad person to acknowledge that. It makes you human.'

He was quiet for a beat. 'So what's making you unhappy, Princess Caroline?'

'Oh, no. You are so not changing the subject like that. Come on. Mum and Dad. What are they like? How did they react to…' she searched for the words to describe what they were doing together '…to Vegas?'

He grimaced; she cringed. 'That bad?'

'They weren't best pleased that we did it without them there. They're hurt, but happy for me. I don't know, but I think that made me feel worse.' He was silent for a moment, fiddling with the label of his beer bottle. 'They want to meet you.'

And she was every bit as terrified of that as he was about meeting her family. She knew that she had a reputation that was about as far as you could get from ideal daughter-in-law. 'I could ask my mother to invite them this weekend? Face everyone at the same time?'

He choked on his beer, caught in a laugh.

'That's sweet, Charlie, but how about we start with introducing them to one royal and go from there. Not everyone is as super cool as me when it comes to meeting you and yours.'

'Oh, right,' she laughed. 'Because you were so ice-cool you practically dropped to one knee the night that we met.'

She wondered whether her tease had gone too far, but his mouth curved in a smile. 'What can I say? You give a whole new meaning to irresistible.'

She could feel herself blushing like a schoolgirl and incapable of stopping it. 'So we see my parents Friday night. Do you want to see yours this weekend too? If you wanted to go sooner I guess I could talk to Rich. Work remotely or something.'

He shook his head. 'Don't worry. I think this weekend will be plenty soon enough. We can fly into Manchester on Saturday. Be back home by Sunday night. No need to miss work.'

'Actually, I could do with stopping by a festival on Sunday, if you fancy it. There's a band

I'd like to see perform, and try and catch them for a chat.'

He nodded, and then Charlie glanced at her watch, realising with surprise that over an hour had passed since they had left the stage. The bar had thinned out a little again, leaving the atmosphere verging dangerously on intimate.

'Speaking of work, I've a fair bit to catch up on. I need to be in the office early tomorrow. Mind if we call it a night?'

He swigged the last of his drink and stood, reaching for her hand as she slipped off the bench. 'I like that you're tall,' he said as they left the bar with a wave to Ruby. 'As tall as me in those shoes.'

'Random comment, but thanks,' she replied, trying to work out if there was a hidden message in there that she wasn't getting. 'Are you just thinking out loud? Is this going to be a list?'

'I'm just...I don't understand. You're right. I didn't play it cool, that night. I didn't play it cool on stage just now. I'm just trying to figure this out. Maybe it is the royal thing, but I didn't struggle not to kiss your cousins when I was at school with them.'

'So you think it's because I'm tall?' Really

thinking: What are you saying? Are you saying you like me? That this is real for you?

'I'm thinking about everything. I just figure that if I can work out what it is…you know…that makes us crazy like that, we can avoid it. Stop it happening again. Keep things simple.'

Her ego deflated rapidly. So it didn't matter what he was feeling, because all he wanted was a way of not feeling it any more. After their madness on stage, they were back on earth with a crash, and she had the whiplash to prove it.

'Well, I'm sorry, darling, but I'm not losing the heels.'

'God, no. Don't,' he said with so much feeling it broke the tension between them. 'I love the heels.'

Which was meant to be a bad thing, she tried to remind herself, but the matching grins on their faces proved it would be a lie.

'Or maybe it's the hair,' he came up with as they walked back to his flat, their fingers still twined. 'There's so much of it. It's wild.'

She tried to laugh it off. 'So we've established you have a thing for tall women with messy hair. I guess I was just lucky I fit the bill.' She turned serious as they reached the front door of the warehouse and stepped into the privacy of the foyer. 'Are your parents going to hate me?'

'Why would they hate you?'

'Notorious party girl seduces lovely northern lad into hasty Vegas marriage. Am I not the girl that mothers have nightmares about?'

'Is that how you see what happened? You seduced me? Because I remember things differently…'

'It's not about what I remember. It's about what your mum will think.'

'My mum will think you're great.' But his tone told her that she wasn't the only one with reservations about the big introduction. 'You'll mainly be busy with dodging hints about grandchildren.'

Her stomach fell and she leaned back against the wall for support while the rushing in her ears stopped.

'She won't seriously be expecting that, will she?'

'She's been bugging me for years about settling down and giving her grandkids. Isn't that what all mums do?'

Apparently they did—that was why she made a point of seeing hers as little as possible.

She drew herself up to her full height again, not wanting Joe to see that there was anything wrong.

'Well, we'll just have to tell her that we don't have any plans.'

Joe was looking at her closely, and she wondered how much he had seen. Whether he had realised that she had just had a minor panic attack.

'It's fine; we'll fend her off together. Are you sure you're okay?'

So he had noticed. She pasted on a smile and pushed her shoulders back, determined to give him no reason to suspect what was on her mind. 'Of course. Just tired. That jet lag must be catching up with me after all.'

It wasn't until she reached his front door that she remembered the whole bed situation. How was she meant to sleep beside him after a kiss like that? After he'd all but told her that he was finding it as hard to resist her as she was to resist him.

She dived into the bathroom as soon as they got into the apartment, determined to be the first ready for bed, and to have her eyes closed and be pretending to sleep by the time that Joe came in. Or better still, actually *be* asleep, and not even know that he was there. She pulled a T-shirt over her head, still warm from the dryer, and gave herself a stern talking-to. She couldn't react like that every time someone mentioned babies or pregnancy. There were bound to be questions after the hasty way that they had got married, and she was going to have to learn to deal with them.

CHAPTER SIX

THERE WAS DEFINITELY something that she wasn't telling him. Something to do with the way that she'd reacted just now when he'd warned her that his mum would probably be hinting about grandchildren.

What, did she already have an illegitimate kid stashed away somewhere? No. It couldn't be that. There was no way that she'd be able to keep it out of the papers. What if she was already pregnant? That could be it. After all, she had accepted a completely idiotic proposal of marriage from a man that she barely knew. Was she looking for a baby daddy, as well as a husband?

And how would he feel if she was? That one was easy enough to answer: as if he was being used. Well, there was nothing new in that. He'd learnt at the age of eighteen, when it transpired that the girl he had been madly in love with at school was only with him for the thrill of sleeping with the poor northern scholarship kid, and bringing him home to upset her parents in front of all their friends, that women wanted him for *what* he was, not who.

And after years on the road, meeting women in every city, every country that he had visited, he knew that it was true. None of them wanted him. The real him. They wanted the singer, or the writer, or the rock star, or the rich guy.

Or—on one memorable occasion—they wanted the story to sell to the tabloids.

Not a single one of them knew who he really was. Not a single one of them had come home to meet his parents. And that was fine with him. Because he knew what he wanted now too. And more importantly he knew that relationships only worked if both of you knew what you wanted—and didn't let emotions in the way of getting it.

But it didn't mean anything, he told himself, Charlie coming home with him at the weekend. Like all the others, she was just using him. He provided a nice boost to her career, and a new way of causing friction with her family, though he couldn't pretend to know why she wanted that. And he was using her to get exposure for his band, and sales for his new album. If he ever finished it.

He tidied up the bedroom while he waited for her to finish in the bathroom, chucking dirty clothes in the laundry hamper and retrieving the rest of Charlie's jewellery from under the bed. They would have to pick up the rest of her stuff from her flat at some point. He'd clear her a space in the wardrobe. Of all the things that he'd thought about that night that they got married, how to manage living with a slob hadn't been one of them. He surveyed the carnage in his apartment, and shrugged. Lucky his housekeeper was going to be in tomorrow. He'd leave a note asking her to clear some space in the drawers and wardrobe.

The thought of it was oddly intimate. Strange, when they were already having to share a bed. Sharing hanging space should have been the least of their worries. But there was something decidedly permanent, committed, about the thought of her clothes hanging alongside his.

It wasn't permanent.

They'd both known and agreed from the start that this wasn't real, and it wasn't going to last. They just had to ride out the next year or so. Let the press do their thing, and then decide how they were going to end things in a way that worked out for both of them. It was as simple as that.

Joe waited outside Charlie's office, wondering whether she'd be pleased or not if he went in. Somehow, over the past three days they'd barely seen each other. That night after the karaoke she'd been asleep by the time that he'd got out of the bathroom, lying on her side on the far side of the bed, so far away that they didn't even need a pillow barrier as a nod to decency. Then she'd been up before him the next morning, though she had said that she had a lot to catch up on. The pattern had stayed the same ever since. She was in the office before he'd had his breakfast every morning, and came home late, clutching bags and suitcases from her flat.

The only sign that they were living together at all was the increasing chaos in his apartment. His housekeeper did her best in the daytime, but once Charlie was home she was like a whirlwind, depositing clothes and hair grips and jewellery on every surface. Leaving crumbs and coffee rings all over the kitchen and the coffee table. He wasn't even mad: he was amused. How had the prim and proper royal family produced such a slob?

It wasn't as if she were lazy. The woman never stopped. He knew that of her reputation at work. That she worked hard to find her artists, and then even harder to support them once they were signed. She was on the phone to lawyers, accountants, artists all day long, and then out at gigs in the evening, always looking for more talent, more opportunities.

Perhaps that was it, he thought. Why waste time picking up your dirty clothes when there was new music to be found?

The pavements started to fill with knackered-looking workers as the clock ticked towards six. As East London's hipster types exited office buildings and headed for the craft-beer-stocked pubs as if pulled by a magnet.

She'd told him she'd arranged for a car to collect her from work and swing by the apartment to pick him up, but as the hours after lunch had crawled by he'd realised that sitting and waiting for her was absolutely not his style.

He strode into the building, mind made up, and smiled at the receptionist.

'Hey, Vanessa. I'm Charlie's husband. Okay if I go straight through?' There. He made sure he sounded humble enough not to assume that she'd know who he was—though he would hope that the receptionist at his own label would recognise him—but confident enough to be assured that he wouldn't be stopped. He breezed past her, wondering why he felt so nervous. All right, he hadn't even visited Afland before, never mind the private apartments at the royal palace, but he had met a fair few royals, between his posh school and attending galas and stuff since his career took off. Deep down, he knew it wasn't who her family was that was making him nervous. It was the fact that he was meeting them at all.

He'd not been home to meet the family for a long time. Not since the disaster with Arabella.

That weekend when he was eighteen, he'd thought he had it made. His gorgeous girlfriend, one of the most popular girls in school, had invited him and a load of their friends to a weekend party at her parents' country house. For the first time since he had started at the school he had felt as if he had belonged. And more importantly had thought it meant that Arabella was as serious about him as he was about her. He'd been on the verge of telling her that he loved her. But as soon as he'd arrived, he'd realised that there was something wrong. She'd introduced him to her parents with a glint in her eye that he knew meant trouble, and had stropped off when they'd welcomed him with warm smiles and handshakes.

Turned out, he wasn't the ogre she'd been expecting them to see. And if he wasn't pissing off her parents, he was no use to her at all. So she'd broken it off, publicly and humiliatingly, in front of half the school and their parents.

Was Charlie doing the same thing? Perhaps marrying him was just one more way for her to stick her middle finger up at her family. Another way to distance herself from her royal blood. But instinctively he felt that wasn't true. Whenever they'd discussed her family, she'd made it clear that she didn't want to upset them. That had been the main thing on her mind that first morning in Vegas. But she hadn't been so concerned about it that she hadn't married him in the first place.

He showed himself through the office, over to where he remembered Charlie's desk was. She couldn't see him approach, her back to him, concentrating on her computer. Her hair was pulled into a knot on the top of her head, an up-do that could almost be described as sophisticated, and a delicate tattoo curled at the nape of her neck. He'd never noticed it before—and that knowledge sent a shudder of desire through him. How many inches of her body were a mystery to him? How many secrets could he uncover if they were to do the utterly stupid thing and give in to this mutual attraction?

They couldn't be that stupid. *He* wouldn't be so stupid. Opening up to a woman, especially a woman like Charlie, was like asking to get hurt.

By the time that he reached her desk, she still hadn't looked up. He couldn't resist that tattoo a moment longer. He could feel the eyes of her co-workers on him, and knew that they were watching, knew that they had read the gossip sites. It was all the excuse he needed, the reminder that he had a part to play.

He bent and pressed his lips to the black swirl of ink below her hairline.

The second that he met her skin a shot of pain seared through his nose and he jumped back, both hands pressed to his face.

'What the h—?'

'What the h—?'

They both cried out in unison.

'Joe?' Charlie said, one hand on the back of her head as she spun round on her chair. 'What were you *thinking*?'

He gave her a loaded look. 'I was thinking that I wanted to kiss my wife. What I'm thinking now is that we might need a trip to A&E.' She looked up then, clocked the many pairs of eyes on them, and stood, remembering she needed to play her part too.

'Oh, my goodness, I'm sorry, darling.' She reached up and gently took hold of his hands, moving them away from his nose. 'Does it still hurt?'

She turned his head one way and then the other, examining him closely as she did so.

'Not so much now,' he admitted, finally making eye contact with her. It was the truth. With her hands gently cupping his face like that, he could barely feel his nose. Barely think about any part of his body that didn't have her soft skin against it.

'No blood anyway,' she added.

He smiled. 'Can't meet the in-laws with a bloody nose and a black eye,' he said. 'Not really the best first impression.'

'They'll love you whatever,' she said, returning his grin, but he suspected it was more for their audience than for him.

She was wearing a black dress, structured and tight, giving the illusion of curves that her tall, athletic figure usually hid. Was this what her parents wanted of her? he wondered. For her to tone herself down and wear something ladylike?

Her phone buzzed on the desk behind her, breaking the spell between them. 'That'll be the car,' she said, gathering up her stuff and shutting down her computer. As she grabbed her purse off the desk she sent a glass of water flying, soaking a stack of scrawled notes.

'Argh,' she groaned, reaching into a drawer for a roll of paper towels. 'Last thing we need.'

'It's fine,' he said, grabbing a handful of the towels. 'Here.' He mopped up the puddle heading towards the edge of the desk and spread out the soggy papers. 'They'll be dry before we're back on Monday. No harm done.'

She blotted at them some more with the paper, glancing at her phone, which was buzzing again on the desk.

'Is it time we were going?'

'Mmm,' she said, non-committal, silencing it. 'It's okay, we've got time.' She started straightening up another stack of papers, and throwing pens in a cup at the back of the desk.

'Wait a minute. Are you tidying?'

She shrugged. 'It's happened before, you know.'

'Maybe, but right now you're stalling, aren't you?'

She stopped what she was doing and looked him straight in the eye, leaning back against the desk with her arms crossing her chest. 'Says who?'

'Well, you just as good as admitted it, actually. What's going on? Ashamed to introduce me to your family?'

She started with surprise. 'Why would I be ashamed?'

'Because you're nervous. Why else would you be?'

'Maybe I'm desperate for them to fall in love with you.'

'Maybe.' He watched her with a wry smile. 'I guess we're going to find out. Are you ready?'

She sighed as she pulled on her jacket and swung her bag over her shoulders. 'Ready.'

As the car pulled through the gates at the back of the palace a few hours later, Joe took a deep breath. He might have been all blasé with Charlie, but now that he was here at the palace, with its two hundred and fifty bedrooms and uniformed guards and a million windows, perhaps he was feeling a little intimidated. Regardless of what he'd thought earlier, his brief brushes with royalty before he had met Charlie hadn't left him at all prepared for this.

Throughout the short flight to the island, he'd been making a determined effort not to feel nervous—forcing his pulse to be even and his palms dry.

And now, as they stepped out of the car and through the doors of the palace, perhaps if he closed his eyes, shut out the scale of the entrance gates, the uniformed staff in attendance, and the police officer stationed at the door, he could almost imagine that this was just any other dinner.

Eventually, following Charlie into the building and through a warren of corridors, he had to admit to himself that there was no escaping it. 'The private apartments are just up there,' Charlie told him as they rounded yet another corner.

He nodded, not sure what the appropriate response was when your wife was giving you the guided tour of the palace she had grown up in. In fact, he'd barely spoken a word, he realised, since the car had pulled through the gates.

The uniformed man who had met them at the door faded away as the policeman ahead of them opened the door. He nodded to them both as Charlie greeted him by name, and Joe followed her through the door. Unlike the corridors they'd followed so far, the interior of the private rooms was simple. Plush red carpets, gilt and chandeliers had fallen away, leaving smart, bright walls, soft wood flooring and recessed lighting.

'It's like another world in here,' Charlie said with a smile. 'My parents had it renovated when we were small. They were doing big repair work across the whole palace, so they took the opportunity to modernise a bit.'

'No chandeliers, then?'

'Not really my mother's style. They keep them in the state rooms for the visiting dignitaries and the tourists. But my parents have always preferred things simpler.'

He followed her down the corridor, and she paused in front of a closed door. 'Ready?' she asked.

He took her hand in his and squeezed. ‘Let’s do it.’

She opened the door into a light-flooded room.

Her parents were seated on a sofa to one side of a fireplace, what looked like gin and tonics on the coffee table in front of them.

‘Oh, you caught us!’ said Queen Adelaide, Charlie’s mother. ‘We started without you. I know, we’re terrible.’ She stood and kissed Charlie on the cheek.

Joe just had time to register the stiffness in Charlie’s shoulders before her mother, Her Majesty Queen Adelaide of Afland, was stepping around her and holding out her hand.

He held his own out in return, but couldn’t find his feet to step towards her. Was it because she was the head of state or the head of Charlie’s family that was making him nervous?

‘You must be Joe,’ Queen Adelaide said, smiling and filling the silence that was threatening awkwardness. ‘How do you do?’

Charlie’s father stepped forward and shook his hand too, but he wasn’t as skilled as his wife at hiding his feelings, he noted. And in his case, his feelings appeared to be decidedly frosty.

'Joe. How do you do?'

He wasn't the only frosty one, Joe realised, watching Charlie as they took a seat on the sofa opposite her parents. Her shoulders were as stiff as he had ever seen them, and her back was ramrod straight. She reached for one of the drinks that had appeared on the coffee table while they were getting the formalities out of the way.

They sipped their drinks as silence fell around them, definitely into awkward territory now. And still a distinct lack of congratulations. Perhaps they were waiting for the others to arrive.

Just as he was taking a deep breath, preparing to dive into small talk, he heard a door open, and the apartment filled with the noise of rambunctious children.

'Grandma! Grandpa!'

The kids barrelled into the room with squeals of excitement. The tense atmosphere was broken, and Queen Adelaide and Prince Gerald beamed with proud smiles and stood to scoop up their grandchildren. But Charlie stayed seated; though she smiled, the expression seemed forced.

Three adults followed the kids into the room.

Joe recognised Charlie's sister and brother-in-law, and a second woman who he guessed must be the nanny. She drifted out of the room after seeing the children settled with book and toys, and Joe shook hands with his new in-laws.

'So, Vegas!' Charlie's brother-in-law said as they all sat down. 'Wish we could have done that. Would have given anything to avoid the circus that we had to endure.'

'Endure?' Charlie's sister, Verity, slapped her husband's leg playfully. 'If that was a circus, I don't know how you'd describe our life now, chasing after these two.' But she smiled indulgently as she said it. Charlie leaned forward and helped herself to her sister's drink, uncharacteristically quiet.

'It was definitely low-key,' Joe said. 'Just us and a couple of friends.' He took hold of Charlie's hand, wondering whether she was planning on checking back in to this conversation again at any point. He withheld the details of the kitschy chapel they had chosen: it had seemed so funny at the time, but less so now that they were facing the consequences of their actions. He looked across at Charlie, and saw the tension in her expression that revealed how uncomfortable she was.

Isn't that what I'm meant to be feeling? he thought. You're back in the bosom of your family. This is meant to be your home, so why are you so uncomfortable?

He was so distracted by wondering what was preoccupying her that he forgot that he had been nervous about meeting the family. Her family were half of the reason he was so sure that this relationship wouldn't work so if it wasn't her family causing the problems, then where did that leave them?

Using one another—that was it. And he knew that he had to keep his head if he was going to stay ahead of the game, make sure that she was never in a position to hurt him.

His thoughts were interrupted by the arrival of Charlie's brother, Miles, who bowled into the room wearing an air of privilege that outshone his exquisitely tailored suit. He greeted Charlie's brother-in-law with hearty slaps on the back—they'd been friends at school, Joe seemed to remember—and then doled out kisses on the cheek to his female relatives.

'So you're the guy who seduced my sister,' he said when he reached Joe.

He gave Miles a shrewd look. Was he trying to get a rise out of him? Well, he'd have to try harder than that.

'I'm Joe,' he said, standing to shake his hand. 'It's good to meet you.'

Charlie had risen beside him and he wrapped an arm around her waist. She seemed calmer with her brother than with her sister. Interesting, Joe thought. Because so far, her brother seemed like a bit of an ass. But families were strange, he knew. Maybe she'd always been closer to her brother. He tried to push it from his mind as they all sat down again. The nanny came back in, then, and the room was suddenly in chaos as toys were put away, negotiations for 'just five more minutes' were shut down and a pair of desultory kids doled out goodnight kisses.

When they got to Charlie, that stiffness came back to her shoulders, and she straightened her spine, sitting beside Joe on the sofa as if she were in a job interview. She sat deadly still as the children climbed up onto the couch, still offering kisses and messing around.

In contrast to all of the other adults in the room, who were joining in with the kids' silliness, Charlie pretty much just patted them on the head and dodged their kisses.

What was her issue with the kids?

There was no getting away from the fact that there *was* something going on. Joe looked over at Charlie's mum and sister to see if they had noticed—looking for any clues to what was going on—but their attention was completely on the children. Joe's earlier suspicion came back to him. Could she be pregnant? Did that even fit with what he was witnessing?

It did if she was in denial, he supposed. If she was pregnant and didn't want to be. Or didn't want to be found out.

Finally, the kids were bundled out of the room by the nanny, and a member of staff appeared with a silver tray bearing champagne flutes and an ice bucket.

'Ah, perfect timing,' Adelaide declared as the glasses were handed round and champagne poured.

The tone of her voice shifted ever so subtly, from relaxed and convivial to something more formal. Maybe more rehearsed. Charlie was close by Joe's side still, and this time it was she who took his hand, and ducked her head under his arm as she wrapped it around her shoulders and turned in towards him, until she was almost surrounded by his body. He tried to meet her eyes, but she evaded him. He couldn't be sure with her avoiding eye contact, but if he didn't know better he'd say that she wanted him to protect her. From her own family? Who seemed—to his surprise—a bunch of genuinely nice people who cared about one another. Her slightly annoying brother aside. It just didn't make any sense. Not unless she was keeping all of them—him included—in the dark about something.

'Joe and Charlie,' Adelaide began, 'I'm so pleased that we are all together this evening. While we can't say that we weren't surprised by your news…' her raised eyebrows spoke volumes about how restrained she felt she was being '…your father and I are delighted you have found someone you want to spend your life with. Now we didn't get to do this on your wedding day, so I'm going to propose the traditional toast. If you could all charge your glasses to the bride and groom. To Charlie and Joe.'

Queen Adelaide took a ladylike sip, while Charlie polished off half her glass and pulled Joe's arm tighter around her.

'Joe, we're absolutely delighted to meet the man who wants to take on, not only our wonderfully wild Caroline, but also her family, with everything that entails. We're always so happy to see our family grow, and, who knows, perhaps over the next few years it might be growing even further.'

From the corner of his eye he saw Charlie flinch, and he knew exactly how she had taken that comment of her mother's, whether it had been meant as a jibe about grandchildren or not. He sipped at his champagne, having smiled and nodded in the right places during Queen Adelaide's speech.

'Are you okay?' he whispered in Charlie's ear when the toasts were done and attention had drifted away from them.

She nodded stiffly, telling him louder than words that she absolutely wasn't.

'Want to try and make a break for it?'

She cracked half a smile. 'We'd better stay. I'd never hear the end of it.'

He wondered if that were true. Charlie's parents looked delighted to have her home. But were they really the types to nag and criticise if she left? They'd welcomed him with good grace in trying circumstances. Perhaps they deserved more credit than Charlie was giving them.

But there was no getting around the fact that she was still on edge, even after all the introductions were out of the way and they were all getting on fine. Which meant there was more to this than just her worrying whether they were going to buy their story.

What if he was right? What if she was pregnant, and was using him? Would he walk away from her? From their agreement? How would that look to the press…?

He suspected there was nothing worse as far as the tabloids were concerned than walking away from a pregnant royal wife.

He still had his arm around Charlie's waist, but he could feel a killer grip closing around him, making it hard to breathe. He'd thought that he'd gone into this with his eyes open. He'd thought he'd known what she wanted from him. Had he been duped again? Was he being used again, without him realising it?

'So, Joe, you were at school with Hugo and Seb, is that right? At Northbridge?' Charlie's brother had come to sit beside them, dragging his thoughts away from his wife.

'Yeah, they were a year or two ahead of me though. You know what it's like at school. A different year could be a different planet.'

'They remembered you, though.'

He heard Charlie move beside him, and, when he glanced across at her, she looked interested in the conversation for the first time since they'd arrived.

'What did they tell you?' she asked, a glint in her eye. 'You have to share. Don't you dare hold out on me, big brother.'

'Oh, you know, the usual. Ex-girlfriends and kiss-and-tells. God, you've let your standards slip, getting yourself hitched to this one.'

'Standards? Really? Who did he date at school?'

'You really want to know?' Miles laughed and rolled his eyes. 'Masochist. Fine, it was Arabella Barclay,' Miles said.

He watched Charlie's reaction from the corner of his eye. It was clear that she knew her, or knew of her.

'Wow. Miles is right, Joe. Blonde, skinny, horsey. If you've got a type, I'm definitely not it.'

Her brother laughed, and Joe resisted the urge to use his fists to shut his mouth.

'Thank God I came to my senses and left all that schoolboy rubbish behind,' he said. Trying not to think of that leggy, horsey girl. Or maybe he *should* be thinking about her. Really, looking back, he owed Arabella a big thank you. She'd done him a favour, teaching him about how relationships *really* worked, rather than the schoolboy idealism he'd had at eighteen.

'Trust me,' Joe said, dropping his arm from Charlie's shoulders to her waist, 'you were everything I didn't know I was looking for.' He closed his eyes and leaned in for a kiss, thinking that a peck on the lips would finish off their picture of newly wedded romance nicely. And banish bitter memories of Arabella into the bargain.

How could he have forgotten? Perhaps his brain erased it on purpose, in an attempt to protect him? The second his lips met Charlie's a rush of desire flooded his blood, and he clenched his fists, trying to control it. To control himself. Was this normal? This overwhelming passion from the most innocent of kisses? He pulled away as Charlie's lips pouted, knowing that another second would lead them to more trouble than he could reasonably be expected to deal with.

Her eyes were still closed, and for the first time since they'd arrived at the palace her features were relaxed. A hint of a smile curved one corner of her lips, and the urge to press just one more kiss there was almost overwhelming.

'Okay, you've proved your point.' Miles laughed. 'I will never mention Arabella again. Or the fact that she's still single and still smoking hot.'

Charlie opened her eyes to roll them at her brother.

'Do you think we can stop trying to set my husband up with his ex?'

Miles held up his hands. 'You're the newlyweds. Your marriage is your own business. I was just providing the facts,'

'Well, as helpful as that is, darling,' Charlie's mother interjected, 'I think we can leave gossip about school friends for another time.'

Joe glanced at Adelaide, and as she met his eye he realised that he had an unexpected ally. He smiled back, curious. Charlie had been so worried about how her parents were going to react that it had never occurred to him that they'd actually be pleased to meet him.

They sat down for dinner in one of the semi-staterooms, and Joe looked around him in awe. Away from the modest private apartments, it struck him for the first time that this really was Charlie's life. She'd grown up here, in this home within a palace. Her life had been crystal and champagne, gilt and marble and staff and state apartments. Carriages and press calls, church at Christmas and official photographs on her birthdays. And she'd walked away from all of that.

She'd chosen a warehouse apartment in East London. A job that demanded she work hard. A 'floordrobe' rather than a maid. A real life with normal responsibilities. It occurred to him that he'd never asked her why. He'd mocked the privileges that she'd been born with, but he'd never asked her about the choices that she'd made.

As the wine flowed and they settled in to what to Joe seemed like a banquet of never-ending courses, Charlie relaxed more. He watched her banter with her brother and sister, and marvelled at the change in her since they had first arrived. When her hand landed on his thigh, he knew that it was all for show. Part of appearing like the loved-up new couple they were meant to be. But that didn't stop the heat radiating from the palm of her hand, or the awareness of every movement of her body beside him.

It didn't stop his imagination, the tumble of images that fell through his mind, the endless possibilities, if this thing weren't so damned complicated.

He wanted her. Could he have her? Could they go to bed, and wake up the next morning and *not* turn the whole thing into a string of complications? Could they both just demand what they wanted, take it, and then agree when it needed to be over?

They shouldn't risk it. He looked down at her hand again and caught sight of the gold of her wedding ring. It would never be that simple between them. They were married. They worked together. There was unbelievable chemistry between them, but that didn't mean that a simple night in bed together could ever be on the cards. They'd acted impulsively once, when they'd decided to get married, and that meant that the stakes were too high for any further slips on the self-control front.

Work. That was what he should be concentrating on. Like the fact that he still hadn't managed to write anything new for the album. He'd told Charlie and her boss that it was practically finished when he'd agreed to sign the contract. It *had* been finished. It still was, he supposed, if he was prepared to release it knowing that it wasn't his best work. What he really needed was to lock himself in his studio for a month with no distractions. Unfortunately, the biggest distraction in his life right now was living with him. And then there was the fact that if he was holed up in his studio, then where was the inspiration supposed to come from? What he'd end up with was an album about staring at the same four walls. What he needed was a muse. A reason to write.

Taking Charlie to bed would give him all the material he needed. He was sure of that. But at too high a cost.

They left the drawing room that night and headed to bed with handshakes and kisses from Charlie's family. Charlie stiffly accepted the kisses from her mother, and she climbed the stairs stiff and formal with him.

Joe watched her carefully as she led them down corridor after corridor, low lit with bulbs that wouldn't damage the artworks. He was vaguely aware of passing masterpieces on his left and right, but his attention was all on Charlie.

'Did you have a good time?' he asked. 'I thought it went pretty well; I liked your family.'

She nodded, staring straight ahead instead of at him. 'They liked you. Even Miles.'

'That's how he acts when he likes someone?'

She huffed an affectionate laugh, and turned to face him. 'I know. He's an idiot. We keep hoping he'll grow out of it.'

'Do you think they bought our story?' he asked. Her eyes seemed to turn darker as she looked ahead again. The sparsely spaced lights strobed her expressions, yellow and dark, yellow, dark.

'I'm not sure,' she admitted. 'But I don't think they're going to call us out on it. My mum already—'

She stopped herself, but he needed to know. 'What?' he asked.

'When I first called and told her what we'd done, she told me that she'd take care of it. If we wanted this marriage to go away.'

'And you didn't take her up on it?'

'We'd already talked about why that would be a bad idea. We made an agreement and I'm sticking to it.'

Her face was still a mystery. She was hiding something else. He knew that she was. Something that meant she was happy with their lie of a marriage rather than the real thing. Maybe he'd shock it out of her with some brutal home truths.

'Charlie, I want you. I know we said that sleeping together would be a disaster. But what if it wasn't?'

She turned to him properly now, her eyes wide with surprise. 'And where the hell did that come from?'

'It needed saying. Or the question needed asking. Maybe it could work. Maybe we could give it a go. I mean, we're acting out this whole relationship, so why not make it that bit more believable?'

'Why not? Do you really need me to list the million reasons it's a horrendous idea? As if our lives weren't complicated enough—you want to add sex to the mix?'

'But that's what I'm saying. Maybe it doesn't have to complicate things. Maybe it would simplify them. We're living together. We're married. We're making everyone believe that we're a couple. I mean, how would sex make any of that more complicated?'

'Because you forgot the most important thing—we're pretending. Yes, we had a wedding, but this isn't a marriage. We're not a couple. We're doing this for a limited time only, and mixing sex in with that would just be crazy.'

'So you don't want to. Fine, I just thought I'd ask the question. Clear the air.'

'Whether I want to or not isn't the issue, Joe.'

'So you do.'

'Urgh.' She threw her head back in frustration. '*Totally* not the point. And to be honest I'm surprised you're asking, because we both know that there's some crazy chemistry between us. We've talked about it before. And at no point has either of us thought that doing something about it was in any way a good idea. I don't know why we can't just drop it.'

'Maybe I don't want to.'

They stopped outside a door and Charlie hesitated with her hand on the doorknob, a frosty silence growing between them. Joe decided to take a punt, knowing that he could be about to set a bomb under their little arrangement. But if she wasn't going to volunteer all the facts, he had to get them out of her somehow. A pregnancy wasn't the sort of thing you could ignore for ever.

'How are you planning on passing me off as your baby daddy, then, if we're not sleeping together?'

Charlie took in a gasp of a breath, and as he watched her straighten her spine he realised that he'd been right about one thing—this was going to be explosive. But a shiver ran through him as Charlie walked into the room and he wondered whether he had just made an enormous mistake.

CHAPTER SEVEN

CHARLIE KEPT WALKING, calm and controlled, past the four-poster bed, trying to cover the typhoon of emotions roiling through her. She stopped when she reached the bathroom, an island of cool white marble after the richness of the bedroom.

'What are you talking about, Joe?'

Her teeth were practically grinding against one another, and she didn't seem to be able to unclench her fists.

'You're pregnant, aren't you?' His voice faded towards the end of the sentence, as if he were already regretting asking. But she didn't care about that, because the grief and pain that she had been holding at bay all night, seeing her sister's happiness with her children, her easy contentment, broke through the dam and flooded her. Winded, as if she'd been punched in the gut, she turned. She retched into the sink, as a week of new pain caught up with her. This had been building since she'd seen the newspaper headline announcing her own imminent engagement. She'd held it at bay, distracted herself with her stupid Vegas wedding and then burying herself in her work. But with Joe's crazy, heartless words—his absolutely baseless accusation—the pain had gripped her and wouldn't let her go.

Joe caught up with her and leaned against the bathroom door frame as she retched, hoping that she wasn't going to get a second look at her dinner.

'Are you okay?'

She threw him the dirtiest look that she could muster before hanging her head over the sink.

'Is it morning sickness?'

It took every ounce of self-control she possessed not to howl like a dog and collapse in a heap on the floor. Instead she forced herself upright, regaining control over her body.

'I. Am. Not. Pregnant.'

She forced the words out as evenly as she could, determined not to give him the satisfaction of seeing how he was hurting her, driving the knife deeper and twisting it with everything that he said.

'Are you sure? Because—'

She broke.

'I'm infertile, Joe. Is that sure enough for you?'

Her spine sagged and her legs turned to jelly as she spoke the words that she'd buried for so many years. She didn't even put out her hands to break her fall. There was no point—what could hurt more than this?

But instead of hitting cold marble, she landed on soft cotton, hard muscle. Joe's arms surrounded her, and her vision was clouded by snowy white shirt. She pushed away, not wanting him here, wanting no witnesses to her despair. But his arms were clamped around her, his lips were on her temple and his voice was soft in her ear.

'God, Charlie, I'm so sorry. I never would have said that if…I didn't know. I'm sorry.'

More murmurs followed, but she'd stopped listening. The tears had arrived. The ones that she'd kept at bay since she was a teenager. That she'd forced down somewhere deep inside her.

They tipped off the mascaraed ends of her lashes, streaking her cheeks, painting tracks down Joe's shirt as he held her tight and refused to let go, even as she struggled against him. Eventually, she stopped fighting, and accepted the tight clamp of his arms around her and the weight of his head resting against hers. She listened to the pulse at the base of his throat, heard it racing in time with her own. And then, as her heaving sobs petered out to cries, and then sniffs, she heard it slow. A gentle, rhythmic thud that pulled her towards calm. They'd slumped back against the claw-footed bath, her legs dragged across Joe's when he'd pulled her close and she'd fought to get free. The shoulder of his shirt was damp, and no doubt ruined by her charcoaled tears.

'You know,' he said eventually, 'we'd be more comfortable in the other room.' Their conversation in the corridor, when he'd oh-so-casually asked if she wanted to sleep with him, felt like a lifetime ago. Surely he couldn't be suggesting…

But he was right. The floor was unforgiving against her butt, and as comfortable as the bath probably was once you were in it, it didn't make for a great back rest.

She stood, pulling her dress straight and attempting something close to dignity.

'Let's just forget this whole conversation.

Please,' she added, when he stood behind her and met her gaze in the mirror.

He crossed his arms.

'I'm not sure that I can.'

'Well, I'm sure that if I can manage not to think about it, you can too.' She didn't care that he'd just been gentle and caring with her. Spiky was all she had right now, so that was what he was going to get. She walked through to the bedroom, her arms crossed across her chest and her hands rubbing at her biceps. She was cold, suddenly. Something to do with sitting on a marble floor perhaps. She climbed under the crisply ironed sheets and heavy embroidered eiderdown, pulling it up around her shoulders in a search for warmth. She figured she didn't need to worry about Joe's suggestion about sleeping together. There was no way that he was going to be interested in her now, with her messed-up mascara and malfunctioning uterus. When she looked up he was still standing in the doorway of the bathroom, watching her. She pulled the sheets a little tighter and sank back against the padded headboard, wondering if he was going to drop the subject.

'So how's that going for you?' he asked eventually. 'Not thinking about it, I mean.'

She shut her eyes tight, trying to block him out. She didn't need him judging her on top of everything else. But he wasn't done yet. 'Because it looks to me like burying your feelings isn't exactly working.'

Throwing the sheets down, she sat up, and met Joe's interested gaze with an angry stare. 'Just because you catch the one time in goodness knows how many years that I let myself think about it and get upset—all of a sudden you're a bloody expert on my feelings.'

'You might not think about it, but that doesn't mean that it's not hurting you.' His voice was infuriatingly calm, just highlighting how hard she was finding it to keep something remotely close to cool. If she didn't get a handle on her feelings, she was heading for another breakdown, and that little scene in the bathroom did not bear repeating.

'God, Joe. Stop talking as if you know me. You know *nothing* about this.'

He came to sit beside her on the bed, and his fingertips found the back of her hand, playing, tracing the length of her fingers, turning them over to find the lines of her palm. 'I know that it's getting between you and your family,' he said at last. 'I know that it hurts you every time you see your niece and nephew. Every time your mother casually mentions grandchildren.'

She looked up from their joined hands to meet his eye. He'd seen all that? 'You think you're so insightful, but an hour ago you thought that I was pregnant,' she reminded him.

He boosted himself up on the bed, and with a huff she scooched over, making room between her and the edge of the bed. He picked up her hand again, and focussed intently on it as he spoke. 'So I misinterpreted the reason you were acting funny. That doesn't mean I didn't see it. That I don't understand.'

'You don't. How could you?' She tipped her head back against the headboard and closed her eyes, wishing that he would just drop this. It wasn't as if it really affected him. He had no vested interest in whether she could procreate. It wasn't fair that he was pushing this when she so obviously didn't want to talk about it.

But if she could admit it to herself, perhaps talking felt almost…good. She realised that there had been a heavy weight in her stomach, sitting there so long that she'd forgotten how hard it had been to carry at first. Over time, she had got so used to the pain that she had lost sight of how it had felt not to have it there.

'I know that you let it push you into doing stuff that you regret. What happened that night in Vegas. Was it something to do with this?'

'I was just letting off steam. Having fun.'

'I don't believe you. I've not known you long, Charlie, but I can see straight through you. If I'd known you better that night I'd never have gone through with it. If I'd been able to see how you were hurting.'

'Hurting? I was enjoying myself. I got carried away.'

'For God's sake. Can you still not be honest with me, even now? I'm trying to tell you that you don't have to bury this any more. That if you want, we can talk about it. But you're trying to tell me you don't even care and I know that that isn't true. This is why you said you never wanted to get married, isn't it?'

She rolled her eyes, and tried to fake a snort of laughter. 'As if I even have to worry about that. Who would marry me if they knew?'

'Is that really what you think?' Pulling back, he put some distance between them so he could look her in the eye.

'It doesn't matter, Joe. I came to terms with it a long time ago. But yes, it's what I think. What would be the point of getting married?'

'I don't know. Speaking hypothetically here…isn't it usually something to do with spending your life with someone that you love?'

She snorted. 'Who knew you were such a romantic? But in a real marriage, sooner or later, kids always come up. Everyone's expecting it. Everyone's waiting for it. When you come from my family, especially.'

'And you're going to let that dictate what you do—who you date. What the great unwashed masses expect of you?'

'It's not just them, though. You don't understand. You don't understand my family. It only exists to perpetuate itself. To provide the next generation.'

'And that's the sort of person you'd want to marry, is it? The sort of person who sees you as a vessel for the next generation? If someone's looking at you like that, Charlie, you need to run, as fast as you can, and find someone who deserves you.'

The fire in his voice and in his expression was disconcerting, so much so that she found that she didn't have a counter argument. Because how could she argue with that? Of course she wanted someone who saw her as more than just a royal baby maker, but that didn't mean that he existed.

Joe's arm came around her shoulders, and she turned in to him, accepting comfort from the one person who could truly offer it. The one person who knew what she was going through—even if he couldn't really understand.

Listening to the rhythmic in–out of his breathing, she gradually felt her muscles start to relax. First her shoulders dropped away from her ears as her own breaths deepened to match Joe's. Then her fingers unclenched from their fists, her back gave out as she let Joe's side take her weight, and then her legs, bent at the knee and pulled up to her chest, tipped into Joe's lap, and were secured by the presence of his hand tucked in behind her knee.

With everything that had been said and revealed in the course of a night, there was no danger of things turning sexy. Charlie could feel that her eyes were swollen, and her skin felt red and tight from tear tracks. She felt anything but desirable. Burying her face in Joe's shirt, she tried to decide what she *did* feel.

Secure.

Anchored.

Not that long ago, an emotional night like this one would have seen her out on the town, running from her problems, looking for a distraction. But tonight, with Joe's solid presence beside her, she was exhausted. And where had running got her over the years anyway? Right back here in the palace, with her problems exactly where she'd left them.

She took a deep breath in, and as she let it go she released the remaining tension in her arms and legs, concentrating on loosening her fingers and toes. Her eyelids started to droop, and she knew that there was no point fighting it. She was going under, and she didn't want to go alone.

CHAPTER EIGHT

CHARLIE SNORED.

As in she was a serious snorer.

As in it sounded as if he were sharing a bed with a blowing exhaust pipe.

It seemed there was no end to the ways that this woman kept on surprising him.

Not that the snoring was bothering him, particularly. After all, there was no way that he was ever going to be able to get back to sleep. Not with the way that she had turned her back to him and scooted in, tucked inside the circle of his arms, and pressing back against him. Every time that he moved away, she scooted again, fidgeting and squirming in a way that was just…too good. So he'd stopped fighting it and pulled her in close, where at least she kept still, and his self-control had half a chance of winning out over his libido.

When they had fallen asleep last night they

had been sitting against the headboard, one of his arms draped loosely around her shoulders. She had been curled up and guarded. Forcing herself into the relaxed state that she couldn't find naturally. He'd felt protective. As if he wanted his arms to keep out all the hurts that seemed to be circling her, waiting to strike. And he'd wanted to get into her head, to show her that the way she saw herself wasn't the way the rest of the world saw her. He certainly didn't see her as damaged goods. As being less than a woman whose insides happened to work differently. But he knew she wouldn't believe him if he told her that.

And more to the point, he didn't want her to think that he had some vested interest in the matter. He'd crossed a line yesterday by suggesting that they sleep together, and, now that he knew how narrow a tightrope she was walking, he felt like kicking himself for adding more uncertainty and confusion into the mix. They weren't going to sleep together. She had been right—it would make an impossibly complicated situation even worse. He didn't want to lead her on. This was a limited-time deal, and it would end when they thought the timing was right for both of their careers.

He wasn't getting involved emotionally—he had known all his adult life that relationships worked best when both parties knew exactly where the boundaries were, exactly what they wanted to get out of it. They would be crazy to go back on those agreements now.

He just had to remind himself that she didn't want that either. She wanted this marriage for what it could do for her career. For the ructions it would cause with her family. And, in light of recent revelations, perhaps she wanted it as a hide-out. An excuse not to meet some suitable guy who might have marriage and babies on his mind.

But that was last night. This morning, 'protective' had well and truly taken a back seat. There were more pressing things on his mind, like the way that her legs fitted so perfectly against his: from ankle to hip they were perfectly matched. Or the way that his arm fitted into the indent of her waist.

Or the fact that if she were to wake up this minute, she'd know exactly how turned on he was, just by sharing a bed fully clothed.

How had his life got so complicated? In bed with a woman he wanted desperately—whom he had already married—but whom he knew he absolutely couldn't have. He cursed quietly, trying to pull his arm out from under her. If he wasn't getting back to sleep, he could be doing something useful, like taking a cold shower and then trying to write.

They were due to fly back to the UK and be up at his parents' house by tea time—they'd made no plans for the rest of the day, and he wondered whether he might be able to find some time alone to work. Last night, Charlie had promised to show him the music room, and the urge to feel the keys of a beautiful grand piano beneath the pads of his fingers had been niggling him since he'd woken. But every time he'd tried to make his escape, Charlie had pressed back against him again and he'd thought…not yet. Just another few minutes.

When she settled, he went for it again, this time pulling his arm out firm and fast, determined not to be seduced into laziness another time. His arm was free at last, and Charlie rolled onto her front, a frown on her face as she turned her head on the pillow first one way and then the other. He felt bad, seeing her restless like that. She had had too little sleep since her overnight stop in Las Vegas, and he knew that for once the black rings under her eyes had nothing to do with eyeliner. He stood watching her for a moment, reminded of that first morning, another night where they had collapsed into bed fully clothed.

He pulled off his T-shirt as he headed for the bathroom, and turned on the shower. He let it run cool before he climbed underneath, concentrating on the sensation of the water hitting his head and shoulders, trying not to think of the beautiful woman lying in his bed.

He wished that they could get out of their second trip this weekend. He wasn't sure that there was a good time to introduce your parents to your fake wife, but he guessed that the morning after a huge row and a heartfelt confession was pretty low on the list. Would Charlie be funny with him this morning? He tried to guess how she would act—whether she'd want to talk more, or pretend that it had never happened and she had never said anything—but had to admit to himself that he didn't even know her well enough to predict that.

By the time that he got out of the shower, she was sitting on the edge of the bed, rubbing at her eyes. So much for some alone time. He secured his towel firmly around his waist before he called out to her.

'Morning.'

Really, was that the best he could come up with? he asked himself.

'Hey,' she said back, tying up her hair and stretching her arms up overhead. 'Have you been up long?'

'Just long enough to shower. I was going to take you up on the offer to play in the music room. Have you got stuff you need to do this morning?'

She frowned, and he realised how that had come across. But was it really so unreasonable of him to tell her that he needed some space? She had no problem with staying at the office late when she didn't want to see him—this was practically the same thing.

'I was just going to chill. Maybe hang out with Miles for a bit. I've not had a chance to do that since we got back.'

He nodded, trying not to show how claustrophobic he was starting to feel. Was this a normal part of newly married life? he wondered. This discomfort with sharing your personal space?

He crossed to the bureau, where he'd discovered their clothes had been unpacked, and pulled on a T-shirt and a pair of jeans. He'd wondered when he first woke up that morning whether she'd be uncomfortable with him today, he'd not expected when he'd been lying next to her that he would be the one trying to put space between them.

But it wasn't about her, or even about him. It was about feeling inspired to write for the first time all week, and wanting to make the most of it before the motivation deserted him again.

'You don't mind, do you, if I go?'

He was already halfway out of the door as he asked the rhetorical question, hoping that he remembered how to find his way back to the room she'd pointed out to him the day before.

When he eventually saw the piano in front of him, he let out a long sigh of relief. Then sat on the stool and let his fingertips gently caress the keys, pressing first one, then another, and listening to the beautiful tone of the instrument. One to one with a beauty like this, he could forget that he had a wife somewhere in this maze of a palace. Forget all of the complications that she had brought into his life.

He ran up and down a few scales, warming up his hands and fingers, trusting muscle memory to conjure up the long-memorised patterns. He'd been no more than a baby the first time he'd played the piano, he knew. Remembering family photos with him perched on his mother's knee as they picked out a nursery rhyme together.

These scales and arpeggios had taken him through recitals and grade exams. From his perfectly average primary school to the most influential and exclusive private school in the country.

They never changed, and he never faltered when he played them. From the final note of a simple arpeggio, his fingers automatically tipped into a Beethoven piece. His mother's favourite. The one that he'd practised and practised until his hands were so sore they could barely move, and he could see the notes dancing before his eyes as he tried to get to sleep. It was the piece that he'd perfected for his scholarship interview. The one that had opened up a new world of possibilities in his career—and had eventually taught him the truth about human relationships. Okay, so he wasn't writing any new material. Not yet. He let the thought go; saw it carried away by the music. Because this was important too, these building blocks of his art and his craft.

He let his hands pick through a few more pieces, and he stretched his fingers, feeling the suppleness and strength in them now that they were warmed up. He placed his tablet on the music stand, flicked through folders, looking for where he'd jotted down ideas for new lyrics and melodies, stored away for future development.

There'd been nothing new added for a while. Lately, when he'd been working on songs for the album, he'd been much further down the line than this. It was ages since he'd been at square one with a song.

He listened to a few snippets of audio that he'd recorded. A few odd words and phrases that had struck him. None of it was working. He'd been right the first time around when he'd chosen other ideas over these. He shut off his tablet and returned his fingers to the keys. It was only since he'd met Charlie that he'd been so dissatisfied with the songs that he'd written before. Why should that be? He tried to reason it out logically. Because maybe if he could work out why he suddenly hated those songs, he could work out how to write something better. He let his fingers lead, picking out individual notes, and then chords, moving tentatively across the keyboard as he experimented with a few riffs.

A combination of chords caught his ear, and he played them back, listening, seeing where his fingers wanted to trip to next. Maybe that was something…it was something for now, at least. He grabbed a guitar from beside the piano and tried out the same chords. Then picked a melody around them. He turned on the recorder on his iPad. He wasn't in a position to risk losing anything that might be any good. He turned back to the piano and tried the melody again, tried transposing it down an octave, shifting it into another key. He crashed his fingers onto the keyboard harder. There was something there, he knew it. Some potential. He just couldn't crack it. He needed to get through to the nub of the idea to find out what made it good. How to work with it to make it great.

He'd just picked up his guitar again, determined to at least make a start on something good, when the door opened behind him. He spun round on the stool and threw an automatic glare at the door.

Charlie drew up short on the threshold.

'S-sorry,' she stammered, and he knew his

annoyance at being disturbed must have shown on his face. 'I brought you a coffee.'

He noticed the tray in her hands and thought twice about his initial instinct to kick her straight out. Maybe he could do with the caffeine, something to get his brain in gear.

'Thanks,' he said grudgingly. 'You can come in—you don't have to stay in the doorway.'

He set the guitar down and turned back to the piano, hoping that she would get the hint, but, instead of hearing the door shut behind him, he was being not so gently nudged to the side of his stool while Charlie held two cups of coffee precariously over the keyboard.

'That sounded interesting,' she said. 'What was it?'

He fidgeted beside her, wishing she'd just go and leave him to it.

'It's nothing. Just playing around with a few ideas. Trying to generate some inspiration.'

She plonked herself down beside him and he held a breath as the hot dark liquid sloshed dangerously close to the piano. Somehow, miraculously, the coffee didn't spill. 'What for?' she asked. 'I thought the songs for the album were all done.'

He shrugged. He really didn't want to go into this now. 'They were.'

'Were?' She finally placed the drinks down on the top of the piano and turned towards him, trying to catch his eye. 'Are they not any more? What happened to them?'

He kept his eyes on the keyboard, his fingers tracing soundless patterns in black and ivory. 'Nothing happened to them. I'm just not sure that I want to include all of them. There's one or two I'm looking at rotating out.' He kept his voice casual, trying not to show the fear and concern behind this simple statement. It didn't work. Charlie's back was suddenly ramrod straight.

'And you're telling me this now? How long have you been thinking this?'

'Are you asking as my wife or as a representative of Avalon?'

'I thought they were the same thing.' The monosyllables were spoken with a false calm, giving them a staccato rhythm. But then she softened, leaned forward and sipped at her coffee, looking unusually thoughtful before she spoke.

'What can I do to help?'

His first instinct was to tell her to leave him

in peace—that was the best thing she could do for him. But the timing of this creative crisis suggested that she was in some way to blame for his current dissatisfaction with his work. So maybe she could be the solution too. 'What about a co-writer? I can call a couple of people. Maybe someone to bounce ideas off.'

'I'm not sure,' he said eventually. 'I was happy with everything before we went to Vegas. I didn't feel like I had to do anything more to it.'

'And now?'

'I don't know. I listened to the demo when we were on the plane. I reckon half the tracks need to go.'

She visibly paled. But to her credit she clearly tempered her response. Regardless of the fact that losing half the tracks would throw a complete spanner into the plan that she and Rich had been working on for recording and releasing the album.

'Can we listen together?' she asked. 'You can talk me through what you're worried about.'

He hesitated. No one outside the band had heard the new tracks. The record companies that had been so keen to fight over them had taken their history of big sellers, and not insisted on listening to the new material. Letting his songs loose on the world was hard enough when he was happy with his work. Letting someone listen to something he knew wasn't right… It was like revealing the ugliest part of his body for close inspection.

But this was what Charlie did. He knew her reputation. He knew the artists and albums that she had worked on. She got results, and her artists trusted her. Maybe he should as well. He'd spent the last week with his head buried in the sand, trying to ignore the problem. It was time to try something different.

He reached for the tablet, ready to cue up the demo, but Charlie stopped him with a hand on his arm.

'Why don't you play?' she asked, nodding at the piano keyboard in front of them. 'One-man show.'

He shrugged. It didn't make much difference to him. The songs weren't good enough, and it wouldn't matter how she heard them.

He rattled through the first bars of a track he picked at random. Trying to show her with his clumsy hands on the keys how far from good the song was.

She didn't say a word as he played, but her

knee jigged in time with the music, and as he reached the middle eight her head nodded too.

He reached the end and looked over at her—ready for the verdict. 'I don't hate it,' she said equivocally. 'Are there lyrics?'

'The chorus maybe. The verses are definitely going.'

She nodded thoughtfully.

'Well, let's hear it before we do anything drastic.'

He returned his hands to the keys and took a deep breath, straightening his back until his posture rivalled hers. He'd been taught to sing classically at school, and there was a lot to be said for getting the basics right.

It had been a long time since he'd sung to someone one-to-one, with just a piano for company. In fact, he couldn't remember ever sitting like this with someone. With so much intimacy.

A lump lodged itself in his throat. Was he really nervous? He'd sung to her the first night that he'd met her. Spotted her on the side of the stage halfway through the gig and made eye contact. Had that been it? The moment that everything had changed for them?

There had been thousands in the audience that night. He'd played at festivals where the audience stretched further than he could see. Just a couple of days ago he'd sung with her in front of a growing crowd of Londoners. It hadn't occurred to him that day to be nervous.

But the thought of singing with her sitting beside him at the piano was bringing him out in a sweat.

She waited, letting the silence grow. Waiting for him to fill it. He pressed a couple of keys experimentally then worked his way into the intro.

Her thigh was pressed against his leg; he felt the pressure of it as he worked the piano pedal. He closed his eyes, hoping that banishing her from at least one of his senses would get his focus back where it needed to be.

He took a deep breath and half sang the first words of the verse. His hands moved without hesitation and he felt his voice grow stronger as he moved from verse to chorus and back again. He winced as he sang the second verse, aware that the lyrics were trite and clichéd.

He'd written about love. Or what he thought love might feel like as a thirty-something. The more he thought about the only time he'd thought he'd been in love, the more uncertain he was that that was what he had really felt for

Arabella. Sure, it had been intense at the time. There were songs that he'd written then that still tugged at the heart strings. But something told him that love was meant to be…bigger than that. The connection he felt with Charlie right this second, for example. That was big. In fact, he couldn't quite decide if it was warm and enveloping big, or heavy and suffocating big. All he knew was that it was scary big. And a million miles from what he had felt for Arabella when he was eighteen.

And of course all that was seriously bad news—because big scary feelings did not make for a happy marriage of convenience. He tackled the middle eight with energy, abandoning his original lyrics, and just singing what came into his head. Trying to lose himself in the notes and not overthink.

He sang the last chorus as if there were no one else listening, new lyrics streaming through him as if he were a vessel for something greater than him.

He let his hands rest on the keyboard when he finished, and kept his eyes locked on them as well. He couldn't let her see. It was too dangerous. Too risky to the arrangement that they had both agreed to. He waited until he could be sure his expression was neutral before he picked up his mug from the table beside the piano and took a sip.

'So?' he asked, not sure that he wanted to know what she thought of it.

'Please, please tell me that's not on the cull list.'

He took a second to really look at her. Her eyes were wide, almost surprised. Her bottom lip was redder and fuller than the top, as if she had been biting on it and had only just let it go. He imagined that if he looked hard enough he would be able to see the shadowed indentation of her top teeth still there. That if he leaned down and brushed his own lips against it it would be hot and welcoming.

'I'm not sure about the first half,' she went on at last, 'but the lyrics in the second? The bridge? That last chorus. That's winning stuff, Joe. That's straight to number one and stay there. That's break the internet stuff. I can't believe you were going to toss that.'

'The first half though.'

'The first half we can fix. Anyone who can write the second half can fix the first, I promise you that.'

He stayed quiet for a long moment. He could

ask himself what had just happened, but the truth was that he already knew. She had happened. She was what was different about his writing. He finally had the inspiration that he needed.

He had no doubt that he still had a lot of work to do, but maybe working with Charlie would be a good thing. It had certainly helped with these lyrics; they'd worked their way into his brain as he was singing, reaching his lips as if he were channelling them, not writing them.

He launched into the opening chords of another song. One he was more sure of. He tweaked the words as he sang, reaching for more unusual choices, to pinpoint emotions he'd only been able to sketch before.

He glanced across at Charlie and she was smiling. A weight of pressure lifted slightly; a measure of dread fell away. They could fix this. Together.

More than anything, this was what really brought it home to him what they'd done. They had tied themselves together in every possible way. His career and his personal life were indivisible now.

For so long 'personal life' had been synonymous with 'sex life'. When Charlie had stipulated *no cheating* he'd known that it was a no brainer. Of course he wouldn't sleep with anyone else. But had he really thought it through? He'd voluntarily signed up for months of celibacy. Maybe years. Perhaps he had assumed unconsciously that 'no cheating' and celibacy weren't necessarily the same thing.

Everything seemed to keep coming back to that question—even though they had agreed right from the start that that wasn't going to happen. And now he had acknowledged that his feelings for her were so much more serious than he had originally thought. Had he really thought the word 'love' earlier?

He finished the song on autopilot and knew from Charlie's expression that she could feel the difference. Her smile was more polite and that sparkle had gone from her eyes.

'Lots of potential in that one,' she said diplomatically. 'Definitely one we can work on.' She glanced at her watch and had a final sip of her coffee.

'I should let you work. Are you sure I've packed the right stuff for your parents' house? Because I can go out and pick something up if I need to.'

'Well, you probably can leave your tiara

here,' he said with a smile, so she knew it wasn't a dig. 'Just something for dinner tonight. Doesn't need to be as fancy as at your place.'

Had he really just referred to the palace they were sitting in as 'your place'? Perhaps he was getting more used to this royal thing than he had thought. Getting used to her.

It was getting harder and harder to remember they were only in this to forward both of their careers. The lines between business and personal were blurring to the point that he couldn't see them any more. And that was dangerous, because the further they moved away from that simple transactional relationship, the more at risk his heart and his feelings would be.

'And make sure you've got something you don't mind getting dirty if we're going to that festival. I'm not going to spend the whole time in VIP.'

She rolled her eyes.

'You so don't need to worry about that.'

CHAPTER NINE

CHARLIE CRAWLED UNDER the duvet and across the tiny double bed until she was almost pressed against the wall. Really, the sleeping arrangements in this marriage kept going from bad to worse.

'Do you think they liked me?' she whispered as Joe unbuttoned his shirt and pulled it back over his shoulders, revealing those tattoos she was still getting to know. He pulled a T-shirt from his bag, and then they were covered again. She almost spoke up and asked him not to, but stopped herself. Cosy sleeping arrangements or not, she had no rights over his body. No authority to ask for a few more minutes to look at his skin.

'They loved you,' he replied, sitting on the side of the bed and pulling off his jeans. 'Of course they did. What did you expect?'

'You know what I expected,' she said, tucking her hand under her pillow and turning on her side to face him. He slid between the sheets and lay beside her, mirroring her posture until they were almost nose to nose in the bed.

'And I told you that you didn't have to worry,' he said, though she didn't quite remember it that way.

Why should she care anyway? In a few months these would be her ex in-laws. She wouldn't ever see them again.

He wondered whether his parents had suspected that there was something off about their relationship. But they had been so distracted by Charlie, and protocol and the whole Princess thing that they hadn't seemed to notice anything.

He could feel the warmth of her under the cool sheets, and for a second was flooded by the memory of waking up with her that morning, with her legs fitting so closely to his. Did she even know what she had done?

'Did you know you're an aggressive spooner?' The question just slipped out of him. She looked shocked for a second, but then had to stifle a laugh.

'What's that meant to mean?'

'It means you were grinding into me like

a horny teenager this morning. I didn't know where to put my hands.'

Her mouth fell open. 'I did not.'

He couldn't resist smiling. 'You so did. Forced me out of bed.'

Not strictly the truth, of course. He'd lain there so much longer than was a good idea, just soaking up the feel of her.

'A gentleman would have moved away,' she said.

'A lady wouldn't have reversed straight back in again every time I did.'

She kicked out at his leg. 'You're totally making this up.'

'Why would I do that?' he asked.

'I don't know. Maybe you want me to do it again.'

'Would you?' The very air around them seemed to be heavy with anticipation as he waited for her to answer.

'I asked first,' she said at last, deliberately not answering his question.

Was she serious? Were they really talking about this as if it might happen? She looked as if she wanted it. Her eyes were wide, her lips moist and slightly parted. One hand was tucked under her cheek and the other below her pillow. He didn't dare look any further down. He'd seen her pull on a pyjama top and shorts earlier, and he knew that gravity would be making the view south of her throat way too distracting. Too tempting.

'Maybe,' he replied at last.

Such a simple word. Tonight, such a dangerous one.

She turned her back to him but didn't make any effort to come closer. Was she testing him? Seeing if she came halfway whether he would come forward the other half.

With her back to him it was safe at last to look down. From where she'd tied her hair in a messy knot, the ink at the nape of her neck, down the length of her long, elegant spine. The tapering of her waist disappeared into the shadows under the sheets.

If he reached for her, would that be the point of no return?

Would the touch of his hand on her waist be the same as telling her that he wanted a relationship? That he loved her?

Were those statements true?

He wanted her. He knew that. That was the easy question. But how many times did he have to tell himself that having sex with the woman pretending to be his wife was a bad idea? That it could never be just sex, because it was already so much more than that.

What would she want from him in return? More than sex meant thinking with his heart, rather than his head, and that had got him badly hurt—and embarrassed—before.

He had tried his hardest to learn his lesson after Arabella, but even that humiliation hadn't been enough for him to spot the woman who was only with him so she could sell his secrets to the highest bidder.

Could Charlie really want him for who he was, rather than what he could do for her?

He couldn't remember ever being more turned on, more tempted than he was right now, but he had to be smarter than that.

Taking what he wanted came with a price tag. But tonight he couldn't be certain what the price was, or whether he would be willing to pay. And so as much as it killed him to do it, he turned over, pulled the duvet high on his chest and squeezed his eyes shut.

He heard a rustle behind him and tried not to imagine Charlie lifting her head from the pillow and looking over at him, wondering what had happened. He didn't want to see her confusion as he cut dead their flirtation. Her head hit the pillow hard, and the duvet pulled across to her side of the bed.

'Night, then,' she said, nicking territory and duvet as she spread out her limbs.

He was so tempted to retaliate. Almost as tempted as he had been to kiss her. To be pulled back into their banter. But he kept silent and still, feigning sleep.

Had she imagined it, last night? she wondered, trying to decide if she should be blaming Joe or her overactive imagination for what had happened. Why, oh, why had she had to be so insistent that they didn't have sex? Because that was where this relationship had been heading, before they were so stupid as to get married.

If they'd done the sensible thing and had a one-night stand that first night, like any self-respecting party girl meeting a rock star, they could be thousands of miles apart and a week into forgetting it all by now. Instead she had been shacked up at her new in-laws', trapped in the world's smallest double bed and ready to explode from frustration.

Surely her imagination wasn't good enough to have imagined that flirtation last night. Joe was the one who had brought up the subject of spooning, and when she'd decided she was so goddamned turned on that she didn't care any more whether it was a good idea or not, and all but wiggled her arse at him, he'd literally turned his back on her—the body-language equivalent of 'thanks, but no thanks'. Only less polite.

So when she'd woken first this morning, there was no way she was going to hang around for him to wake up and rehash the whole thing. One rejection was plenty, thanks. She'd known as soon as she told him about her infertility that she was taking herself well and truly off the market as far as he was concerned. It had been stupid to expect any other reaction to her advances than the one that she had got.

So she'd got up and found Joe's mum already in the kitchen, and before she quite knew what was happening there was a cup of strong tea in front of her and the smell of bacon coming from the stove.

'Did you sleep well, then, love? Oh, I shouldn't ask that really, should I? Not to a newly-wed. And that bed in there's so small. Not even a proper double. Hardly room to—'

'Shall I put the kettle on?'

Charlie breathed a deep sigh of relief—not

the emotion she'd expected to feel when setting eyes on Joe that morning. He leaned in the kitchen doorway, colour high on his cheeks as he crossed his arms and gave his mum a look.

'No need, love.' His mum bustled round, pouring another cup from the pot and setting it on the table for Joe.

'I was just saying to Charlie—you are sure it's okay for me to call you Charlie?' She didn't stop for an answer. 'I was just saying that the bed in your room. It's hardly big enough for you on your own, never mind for the two of you great tall things. We'll have to do something about that. Maybe you should have our room.'

Joe kissed his mum on the cheek and extracted the tongs from her clasped fist.

'You're babbling, Mum. Sit down and drink your tea.'

His mum sat and he shot a glance over her head to Charlie, who smiled conspiratorially in return.

'You sure you don't want to come with us today, Mum?' Joe asked as he served up the bacon sarnies.

'Me in all that mud? You must be mad, love.'

'Mud? It's twenty-five degrees outside. Not

every festival is Glastonbury in the rain, you know.'

'I've seen these things on the telly, love. Maybe if you were playing, but I'll give it a miss. You two love birds don't want me and your father there playing gooseberry anyway.'

Joe rolled his eyes as he picked up a sandwich, 'Mum, there'll be thousands of people there. It's not like we're expecting to be alone.'

'Don't be obtuse, Joe. You know full well it's not the same.'

'I feel awful shooting off like this,' Charlie said. They'd sat down to dinner barely an hour after they had arrived last night, and she'd been so beat after four courses and dessert wine that they'd retreated to bed long before midnight.

'Don't be daft, love. You young people are so busy, and Joe's already told me how hard you work.' Interesting…when had he told her that? 'It's been lovely that you made it up here with everything that you've both got going on. Don't go and spoil it by overstaying your welcome.'

Charlie smiled, surprised by how at home she felt with Joe's parents already. As if she really were becoming part of the family. Probably best that they were leaving this afternoon, then. Before this became another reminder of how hard it was becoming to keep reality and pretence straight in her head.

They climbed into Joe's car, chased by kisses and offers of baked goods for the journey. The festival was out in the countryside, about half an hour from his parents' house. Thank God it was no further, Charlie thought, twenty minutes of isolated confinement later. There was a limit to the tension that her body could take, and she was rapidly approaching it.

They were going to have to talk about what had happened last night. She'd hoped that maybe they could just ignore it—forget it had happened. And then his mum had been so funny with her babbling that she'd thought that they'd taken a shortcut and moved past it. But after breakfast they had been back in Joe's tiny bedroom, trying to pack their bags without touching. Moving around each other as if they were magnets with poles pointing towards one another. And she knew it would take next to nothing for those poles to flip and they would be back where they had been last night, drawn together, with only their self-control and better judgement fighting against the inevitability of the laws of nature.

She rested her chin on her hand; her elbow propped on the door as she gazed out of the window. They had barely spoken a word since they'd climbed into the car.

'Have you played here?' Charlie asked, needing the tension broken—before it broke them. The question counted as work. Talking about the band and work was safe. It was the only safe zone they had.

'Two years ago,' Joe replied, his eyes still locked on the road. They hadn't left it for a second since they'd left his parents' driveway. 'Were you here?' he asked.

'Yeah, with one of my artists. I didn't see you.'

'I wonder how many times that's happened,' he said, and for the first time he glanced over at her.

She furrowed her brow. 'That what's happened?'

'That our paths have crossed and we've not seen each other.' His eyes were back on the road now, but he looked different somehow, as if he was having to work harder to keep them there.

She tried to keep her voice casual, not wanting to acknowledge the way the tension had just ratcheted up another notch. 'I don't know. Must be loads if you think about it.'

'I can't believe it,' he said.

She looked over at him again, to find him watching her. They'd pulled up at a junction, but his attention was all on her, rather than looking for a gap in the traffic crossing their path.

'Why?'

'Because...*this*. Because of the atmosphere in this car for the last twenty minutes. Because of how it felt in Vegas, knowing that you were watching me. I just can't imagine being in a room with you and not feeling that you were there.'

How *what* had felt in Vegas? She thought back to that moment when she was watching him from the side of the stage and their eyes had met. He had felt that too?

He reached for her hand. She considered for a split second whether she should pull away. It was what he'd done last night. She'd reached out to him, and he'd known it was too dangerous. A bad idea.

Could she be as strong as he had been?

His hand cupped her cheek, and she knew she could. She could be strong and resist, as he had. But maybe she could be a different kind of strong. Maybe looking at all the reasons this was a bad idea, all the reasons it was a terrifying choice, and *still* choosing it, maybe that was strong too.

She leaned forward across the centre console, sliding her hands into his hair and bringing their mouths together.

Her body sighed in relief and desire as his tongue met hers, simultaneously relaxed and energised by this feeling of…perfection. This was it. This sense of fitting together.

A horn blared behind them and she sprang back, reeling from her realisation.

He grimaced as he slid the car into gear and pulled away, with just a slight lurch as the clutch found its biting point. This was what she'd been waiting for; and it was what she'd been dreading. She'd been running from it her whole adult life. She didn't want to be completed. She didn't want to belong with someone. Her one-off dates and casual boyfriends—she never had to tell them she was infertile. Never had to spell out the future that they would never have. Never had to explain that if she shacked up with someone long-term and the babies didn't come that they'd be hounded by the press and his virility would be called into question. Their bins would be searched and their doctors harassed. Her body had been public property since before she was born. Anyone who wanted to spend their life with her would be volunteering for the same deal—who in their right mind would do that?

Ten more minutes. She had to survive just ten more minutes in this space with a man she was finding it impossible to remember to resist. They showed their passes at the gate and, in silence, Joe directed the car through the gates and down a rucked track towards the VIP parking, waved along by marshals. When they arrived, Joe pulled on the handbrake and opened the door, while she gathered her things from the footwell. Her door opened, and Joe was there, holding out his hand like a cartoon prince.

'Very gallant,' she said lightly, knowing that her confusion was causing a line to appear between her eyebrows.

He handed her down from the car, and as her feet reached the ground he pressed her back against the rear door, one of his knees nudging between hers. His hand caught at the ends of her hair and he pulled gently, bringing a gasp of pleasure and anticipation to her lips. She tilted her head to one side as she met his eyes, and saw passion and desire. Another inch closer and she was trapped. Car behind, hard body in front, and still that hand in her hair, pulling to one side now, exposing the pulse of her throat. She licked her lips in anticipation and closed her eyes as Joe moved closer. First cool lips descended and then a flicker of warm tongue in a spot that made her shudder. The butterfly caresses of his mouth traced up the side of her neck, then suddenly down to her shoulder, where her shirt had slipped, exposing her collarbone. The sharp clamp of his teeth on her sensitive skin made her gasp in shock. But the noise was lost as his lips were suddenly on her mouth, and his tongue was tangling with hers.

She wound her fingers in his hair, levering herself a little higher, desperate to bring their bodies in line. Cursing her decision to wear flat biker boots instead of her usual heels. Who cared about practicalities when there was a man like this to kiss?

Joe pressed into her with an urgency she'd not felt from him before. An urgency that made her wonder how spacious the back of his car was, and how much faith they wanted to put in the tinted windows.

It was as his lips left hers, to dip again to her neck, that she heard it.

Click.

Her eyes snapped open and she pushed at Joe's chest. She didn't have to look far over his shoulder to see the photographer. She took a second, breathing heavily and trying to remember that she was meant to be pleased about the press involvement in her life for once, before she spoke.

'You knew he was there?' she asked quietly, her lips touching Joe's ear. Her calves burned as she stretched up on tiptoes, but she wasn't ready to back down, back away, just yet.

'Spotted him as I got out of the car,' Joe whispered back.

Which explained the little display he'd just put on, then. Thank God she hadn't suggested taking the party back into the car.

'You okay?' he asked, and she forced a smile, pushing slightly on his chest and trying to regain her equilibrium. Desperate for a balance between trying to convince the photographer that that kiss had rocked her world, and not letting Joe see the truth of it.

'I'm fine.'

Their encounter with photographers at the airport seemed a long time ago and a long way away. She'd barely noticed over the past week that they hadn't been harassed by the paparazzi as much as she'd thought they might be—perhaps her mother had had a discreet hand in that. But there was no way that even her mother could keep them away here. The reality of the situation struck her—something she'd not counted on when she and Joe had been making plans for seeing family and work: they were going to be on display, all day. They couldn't afford to slip up. She closed her eyes and kissed Joe lightly on the mouth, telling herself it was just her way of warming up for the performance she knew that they had to nail.

'Want to go listen to some music?' she asked.

'No,' he said with a smile. 'I want to stay here and kiss you.'

She couldn't help grinning in return, not even trying to work out if it was for real or for show. Leaning back against this car in the sunshine, kissing a super-hot guy—that sounded pretty good to her too. But the moment was gone, and she couldn't lose the photographer from the corner of her eye.

'You're so going to get me fired,' she said. 'I'm meant to be working.'

'Well, then, jump to it, slacker. I'm not going to be one of those husbands who expects you to stay home and play house. Get out there and earn your keep.' He took a step back from her, and she slid her hands behind her butt. She knew real life was waiting for them, but what was just a few more minutes?

'I'd make a lousy housewife.'

'Oh, I don't know,' he said with a laugh. 'Some people like the hovel look. I hear it's big this year.'

She poked him in the ribs and laughed back. 'I'm not that bad.'

'You're worse.' He turned and stood beside her, draping a casual arm around her shoulder and pressing a kiss to her temple.

It would be too easy to take this little scene at face value, she knew. A week ago she'd be giving herself a stern talking-to. That all this was for the benefit of the photographers and the eager public. But today...today the line was more blurred. Her first thought had been that Joe was just putting on a show, but they had been moving so much closer for the last few days that she knew that some part of it was real. Their performance, it didn't feel like some random invention—it was more… Maybe it was what their relationship might have been if their lives were simpler. If she weren't a princess with a wonky reproductive system. If he formed actual emotional relationships rather than using women to get what he needed. Would it work? she couldn't help but wonder. If they had been two ordinary people, with ordinary lives, would they have been happy together?

'Come on, then,' she said at last, pushing herself away from the car, trying to shake the thought from her mind. It didn't matter if it would work that way, because they weren't those people, and never could be. Joe moved with her, his arm still around her shoulders as they made their way into the festival.

As Joe had promised, they were in the VIP zone for no more than half an hour before she was dragging him through a dusty field of festivalgoers, littered with abandoned plastic cups. She refused to watch the band from the side of the stage—she wanted the full experience, to see what she would be working with if she ever got this band to agree to sign with her.

The Sunday afternoon vibe was chilled and relaxed, with families dancing to the music, kids on shoulders, or eating on picnic rugs on the ground. Groups of people sat on the floor, passing round cigarettes and bottles of drink.

The sun was hot on her back, and she was pleased she'd pulled on one of Joe's long-sleeved shirts with her denim shorts, protecting her shoulders from burning.

For a while they just wandered, soaking up the atmosphere of a group of people united by a passion for music. Joe's fingers were loosely wound between hers, keeping her anchored to him. To their story. The impression of that kiss was still on her lips, and had been refreshed every now and again with a brief re-enactment. They couldn't just keep an eye out for cameras and people watching. For the first time since they had arrived back in the UK, they were truly having to live out their fake marriage in full view of the public.

And the weirdest part…it wasn't weird at all. In fact, it felt completely natural to be walking round with her hand in his. The way he threw an arm over her shoulders if they stopped to talk to someone. For once, she decided she actually liked being in flat shoes. Liked that his extra height meant that she was tucked into his body when he pulled her to him. It felt good—warm, safe, protected. Everything she'd been telling herself she didn't want to be.

'Want to find something to eat?' Joe asked when the band they had been watching finished.

'Dirty burger?' she asked, with a quirk of her brow.

'Whatever turns you on.'

You know what turns me on. The response was right there on the tip of her tongue, but she held it back, not trusting where it might lead them.

'Come on,' she said, pulling him towards a van selling virtuous-looking flatbreads and falafel. 'These look amazing. I'm having a healthy lunch, then I'm going in search of cider.'

With lunches in hand, they picked their way across to another stage, where Casual Glory, the band Charlie wanted to see, were just warming up at the start of their set.

'I saw these guys in a pub last year,' she told Joe. 'I wanted to sign them then and there. But then all the suits got involved and…I don't know, maybe they got spooked but somehow it didn't come off. I don't want to let them out of my grasp again.'

'They're still not signed?' Joe asked.

She dropped to the floor and sat cross-legged, watching the band while she ate.

'Free spirits. Didn't like the corporate stuff. And I'm not sure what I do about that, to be honest, because the music business doesn't really get much more laid-back than with Avalon.'

'You think you can get them to change their minds?'

Charlie nodded. 'I'm going to. I'm just not sure how yet.'

'You're not going to marry him, right?'

She laughed under her breath.

'One husband's already too many, thanks.'

He wound an arm around her neck, pulling her close and planting a kiss on her shoulder.

'You're right: they're good,' Joe said after they finished another song. 'Loads of potential. You should bag them.'

'Yeah, well, try telling them that,' she joked.

'I will, if you want. Are we going to say hi when they're done?'

'That's the plan.'

She leaned against his shoulder, soaking

up the sun warming the white cotton of her shirt. Her head fell to rest against Joe's and she shut her eyes so she could appreciate the music more.

'Tired?' Joe asked in her ear, and she 'mmm'ed in response. She couldn't remember the last time she'd had a properly restful night's sleep. Turned out being married was more likely to give you black bags than a newly-wed glow.

'Come here, then.'

Joe pushed her away for a moment, then slung his leg around until she was sitting between his thighs, her back pulled in against his front. She relaxed into him, shutting out all thoughts of whether this was a good idea or not. Just letting the music wash through her. Soak into her skin and her brain.

'Comfortable?' Joe whispered in her ear.

'Too comfortable.'

She felt more than heard him chuckle behind her as his arms tightened. A press of lips behind her ear. A kiss on the side of her neck. A tingle and a clench low in her abdomen: a silent request for more and a warning of danger ahead.

Instead of heeding it, she let her head fall

to one side, just as she had done by his car. They were in public, she reasoned with herself. There was only so far this could go. It was all a part of their performance.

'How about now?' he asked, pulling her hair over to her other shoulder. 'Feeling sleepy still?'

God, he was driving her insane.

'Like I could drop off at any moment.'

He growled behind her and she smiled, revelling in the way she was learning to push the boundaries of his self-control. His hand in her hair was tough and uncompromising now, and she let out a gasp as he pulled her back slowly, steadily, never so hard that it hurt. Making her choose to come with him rather than forcing. She opened her mouth to him without question. The hand still round her waist flattened on her belly, pressing her closer still.

She let out a low sigh of desire and her arm lifted to wind round his neck, opening her body. Was Joe controlling her without her realising? She didn't remember meaning to do it. Then his hand dropped from her hair and cupped her jaw: the kiss gentler now, sweeter.

She opened her eyes and smiled back at him, and she knew her eyes must look glazed, dopey. 'All right, I'm not likely to sleep in the next year. Is that what you wanted?'

'I'll take it,' he said with a smug smile. She leaned back into him again, languor and desire fighting to control her limbs.

CHAPTER TEN

'I WISH WE didn't have to go back tonight,' Joe said, stretching out his legs and leaning back on his elbows. Maybe it was the sun making him lazy, making him feel that he never wanted to leave this place. Charlie moved so she was lying to one side of him, her head propped on her hand.

'I thought you'd be dying to get back in your studio,' she said. 'You seemed all…inspired and stuff yesterday.'

'I am. I do want to write.' He'd had ideas swirling round his brain for two days; when they'd been at his parents' house he'd been desperate for a bit of space and time to try and get them down on paper, or recorded on his phone. But since they had arrived at the festival, since that kiss, everything felt different. 'I can't remember the last time that I was relaxed like this. The last time I felt still. I like it.'

'You can be still in London,' Charlie said.

He shrugged—or as best he could with his body weight resting on his elbows. 'I don't know if I can. Or maybe it's that I know that I won't.'

She sat up and gave him a serious look. 'Not every day can be Sunday afternoon at a festival. Real life is still out there, you know.' Of course he knew, but somehow he was managing not to care.

'I do know. But it feels that it can't get us here.'

'What are you worried about "getting us"?' she asked.

Why did they have to think about that now? Why couldn't they just enjoy this? He wished he knew. He'd just told her he felt still—what he'd wanted to say was that he felt happy. Content. He'd wanted to say that he'd stopped trying to work out if what she was saying was loaded. A way to get something more than they'd agreed from their arrangement.

Here at the festival, life was simpler. He could kiss and touch her. Laugh with her. Treat her as the woman he was in love with. No holding back.

Was that really it? Was that what was making him feel so…serene? Because he didn't have to pretend not to love her?

His phone chirped and he fished it out of his pocket, grateful for the distraction from his own thoughts.

'Amazing, they're here. Some friends of mine have stopped by,' he told Charlie. 'Want to say hi after you've done your work stuff?'

'Sure, why not? Who are they?'

'Owen's band supported us at a couple of gigs a few years ago. We hung out a bit. His wife's lovely too. You'll like them.'

He stood and pulled her up as Casual Glory finished their final number. His arm fell round her shoulders in that way that felt so completely natural. Perhaps it was just their height, he thought. He'd told her that he'd liked that she was so tall, but her flat biker boots today meant that he was a few inches taller than her. Or maybe it was something else—something to do with escaping their real lives and real pressures. They were meant to be putting on a show to the public today—but in reality it had given them permission to stop pretending for the first time since they had woken up married.

They passed through security to the VIP

area, and Charlie headed straight for the lead singer of Casual Glory and gave him a hug. Joe hung back a little, watching her work, impressed. She didn't just schmooze—though she did compliment them on their awesome set. She also challenged them, asked them about their goals and their hopes for the future. Showed them subtly that she would be their ally if they wanted to make that a reality. And she made sure that each member of the band left with her business card in their pocket and some serious thinking to do.

Charlie cut the conversation short before they outstayed their welcome, and they headed over towards the bar. He surveyed the room once he had a jar of craft cider in hand—it was full of people resting their feet, snatching glasses of free champagne, and trying to get a sneaky snap of the VVIP whose hen do was in full drunken flow in the corner.

He tapped the side of his glass, wondering whether he had missed his friend, and whether they should commandeer one of the golf buggies to go in search of him when he recognised Owen's shaggy, shoulder-length hair and waved at him from across the crowd, squeezing Charlie's hand at the same time. He wondered for a split second whether he had done the right thing in looking Owen up, but it was too late to back out now. Owen turned and saw him, waving from across the tent.

'Hey,' Joe called out, making a move towards his friend.

Charlie followed the direction of Joe's wave and saw Owen—she recognised him from a gig she'd been to last year. And then a blonde woman—polished and beautiful—stepped from behind him, a chubby baby settled on her hip. Charlie's stomach lurched and she felt bile rise in her throat. Joe should have warned her.

He was the one who had called her out on how uncomfortable she had been acting around her sister and her kids. He had to know just how hard this would be for her. Especially with the way that talking about everything had been tearing open old wounds recently.

She realised that she'd come to a halt, and only Joe's hold on her hand pulled her forwards.

'Owen, hey, man. Alice, you look gorgeous.' Joe shook his friend's hand and kissed Alice's cheek. 'Guys, this is Charlie.' He'd pulled her to him and wrapped his arm around her waist. He was putting her through this and he didn't even care—didn't even think to try and understand how much this was hurting her.

Alice leaned in and kissed her cheek and Owen shook her hand.

'Congratulations, you two!' Alice said with a friendly smile. 'I can't believe someone's tied this guy down. You deserve a medal, Charlie. I can't wait to hear all the details.'

Charlie tried to return her smile, but felt her facial muscles stiffen into a grimace.

'And who's this?' Joe asked, chucking the baby's cheek and being rewarded by a belly laugh. 'Looks like we should be the ones saying congrats.' Charlie sensed something slightly forced in his cheerful tone. What was he up to?

'This is Lucy,' Alice said, and shifted the baby to hold her out to Joe. 'Want to hold her?'

'Are you sure?' He took the baby awkwardly and held her up to his face, pulling funny faces. Joe with a baby. Charlie watched him closely, trying to work out what he was feeling. His smile was open and straightforward, and she envied him for it. She wished she could enjoy the sweet, heavy weight of a baby in her arms without being haunted by the inevitable regret and sadness.

'That must have moved quickly, then,' Joe was saying. She struggled to follow the conversation—feeling as if she had missed some vital part. 'The last time I saw you, you were still mired in bureaucracy trying to bring this one home.'

'Our social worker was awesome,' Alice replied. She turned to Lucy with another megawatt smile. 'We've adopted Lucy,' she said.

And the bottom fell out of Charlie's stomach. She stumbled, and the only thing to grab hold of to stop her falling was Joe. Again, goddamn him.

Had he planned this? Manipulated her into meeting this gorgeous family, with their beautiful baby?

Of course he had—that was what she'd heard in his voice. He'd been planning this behind her back. So after everything he had said about her being enough for any man just as she was, and it didn't matter if she could have children or not, here was the proof that he felt otherwise. She'd always known that it was always going to be true in the end.

It was as if he'd not listened to a word she'd said since they'd met. As if he didn't know her.

'L-lovely to meet you,' Charlie managed

to stammer, and then she turned and started walking. She didn't even care where she was going. She just had to get out of there. Away from Alice and her gorgeous baby. Away from Joe and his lies and manipulations.

She reached sunshine and fresh air but kept walking, wanting as much distance as she could get between her and Joe. She couldn't remember where the car was so she just walked out. Out as far as she could. Tears threatened at the edges of her eyeliner, but she knew that she must not let them fall. Even now, they had to make this deception work, or what had been the point of any of it? She spotted the VIP car park and headed towards Joe's car. She just wanted to not be here.

The keys. Damn it. Well, maybe there would be someone else leaving and she could hitch a ride—

'Charlie!'

She recognised Joe's voice, her body responded to it—to him—immediately, but she fought it and kept walking. He couldn't possibly have anything to say to her that she would want to hear.

'Charlie, stop. Please!'

Ahead of her, someone was staring at them.

She wanted so much not to care. To be a nobody—unrecognisable in a crowd. Someone no one knew or cared about. But she stopped, because she wasn't that person. She could never be that person.

Joe caught up with her, rested his forearms on her shoulders. God, if he asked her what was wrong, that was it. She was running and crying and she didn't care who saw.

'I'm sorry,' he said. 'I should have warned you that they have a baby.'

She shrugged his arms off her shoulders. He was trying, but he still didn't get it. 'I'm not angry about the baby, Joe. Babies don't make me mad. I'm angry because you tried to manipulate me.'

'Manipulate you? How?'

He'd raised his voice, but then looked around. Remembered where they were.

'Maybe we should talk about this in the car.'

She narrowed her eyes. Right—they needed to protect their secret. He climbed into the car and she sat on the passenger seat, looking straight out ahead, not able to face looking at him properly.

'I should have warned you about the baby,' he said again. 'But I thought I was doing something good. I thought seeing how happy they are to have her would help. That they're a family, even if not by conventional means.'

'So what are you telling me—you want to adopt a kid? Is that your next big idea? Your next publicity campaign? It doesn't matter that I'm damaged goods, because you can always stick a plaster on that?'

'Don't be ridiculous, Charlie. This isn't about me and you know it.'

'Oh, of course, because all this is just for show. It's all about your career.'

'Yours too,' he bit back. 'You make me out to be mercenary, but don't pretend that you're not using me every bit as much as I'm using you.'

He was using her.

Of course he was, she had known that from the start. But to hear him say it like that—no sugar coating—it winded her. And he thought that she was just as bad as him. That she had made a cold, calculated decision to use him. Well, she couldn't let him go on believing that. She wasn't that much of a bitch.

'My career? You know that that wasn't why I married you. Unlike you, I'm not that mercenary. I saw a headline in the news, that night. My parents trying to marry me off to one of those suitable husbands who'd be waiting for his heir and spare. I married you because my family were trying to force me into being the happy wife that I knew I never could be. When I have reminders of my infertility thrust in my face, Joe, I have been known to go a little crazy and act out. I could see the life I had built for myself slipping away and I was so heartbroken I couldn't think straight. That doesn't make us the same.'

CHAPTER ELEVEN

'You were still using me,' Joe said. Charlie rolled her eyes at him, but he was still reeling.

'Oh, because you're such a goddamn expert, are you?' she said. 'Is it all women that you know so well, or is it just me? Because I've been on your telly and in your newspapers my whole life you think you know what I'm feeling.'

'I never said I think I know you—but I think I know something about women. About relationships. I do have some experience of this.'

'Oh, so we're finally going to get to the bottom of this. Good. It was Arabella, I assume, who broke your heart.'

'Nobody said my heart was broken.'

'You scream it without saying a word, Joe. You with your trust issues and fear of commitment. You've already seen every article of my dirty laundry. Are you going to tell me what went on to make you such a cynical son of a b—? Or are we going to carry on trying to work out what's going on with us while having to avoid stepping on the elephant in the room?'

He slapped the steering wheel. Why was she so determined to make this about him—to make him the bad guy? He had been trying to help, and now she wanted to drag up his past as if that had anything to do with what they were arguing about. 'There is no elephant. Arabella and me—it wasn't a big deal. I wasn't heartbroken. If anything I'm grateful to her. She taught me a lot.'

'Like what?'

'Like how relationships actually work—and I don't mean the hearts and flowers rubbish. I'm talking about real adult relationships where both partners are upfront and honest about what they expect.'

'And let me guess, what Arabella expected wasn't just to enjoy your company. What else did she want?'

He tried to wave her off, but he knew that she wasn't going to let this drop. The fastest way out of this argument was just going to be to tell her the truth. Then she'd see that Arabella had nothing to do with any of this.

'She wanted to piss off her parents. She thought that taking me home to meet them would do that.'

Charlie raised her brows. 'And when did you find this out?'

'When we turned up at her house for the weekend. They were perfectly nice to me and Arabella was furious. I think that she thought that one whiff of my accent and they'd be threatening to disinherit her. She'd read too much D H Lawrence.'

'And before that… Were you in love with her?'

He shrugged, because what did it matter how he had felt when he was a naïve eighteen-year-old?

'Before that, I thought things were as simple as being in love with someone. I know better now.'

'That's a pretty cynical way to go through life.'

'Is it? Are you telling me that if you meet a guy you love you'll just marry him—no thinking about real life, your family, your career? Children?'

'I married you, didn't I?'

He didn't know what he could say to that.

She had just told him that she hadn't been thinking straight. Surely she couldn't be saying that she loved him. But she didn't deny it either. He shook his head—he had to try and make Charlie understand how Arabella had helped him. That he was happy with his life as it was. Or he had been, until he had met her.

'All I know is that since Arabella, I've not been hurt,' he said. 'Someone tried. Pretended that she wanted me, when all she wanted was something she could sell to the papers. If I'd not learnt my lesson after Arabella, maybe that would have affected my heart too. But I'm a quick study.'

Charlie reached for his hand and absent-mindedly traced the lines of the bones beneath the skin. He tried not to notice, tried not to feel that caress in the pit of his stomach. She was still looking out of the window, and he was cowardly grateful that she wasn't making him do this eye to eye.

'And is that what you want from life?' she asked. 'From the women in your life—just to not get hurt? Or, one day, are you going to want more than that? Are you going to want to risk going all-in? Risk your heart, and see what you get back.'

He let his head fall back against the head rest, and let out a long, slow breath. 'I don't know, Charlie. What could be worth that?'

She turned to face him, and he knew that she was not going to put up with his evasion any more. That all pretence that they were not talking about them now was flying out of the window.

'Are you serious?' she said, her eyes blazing. 'Don't you think that this could be worth it? That *I* could be?'

Her expression was wide open—she was holding nothing back, now. No more secrets. Nowhere left to hide.

'This was meant to be all for show,' he said.

'And yet here we are. We both know we didn't go in to this for the right reasons, Joe. But the more time we spend together, the more I feel this…this pull between us that I've never felt before. And I don't know what to call it. I'm scared to call it love, but nothing else seems to fit.'

'But what do you *want*, Charlie?'

'For God's sake. Why do I have to want anything, Joe, other than you? Why can't you believe that that's enough? I want what we had last night, whispering and laughing in bed together. I want yesterday, at the piano, feeling like I can see into your soul when you play and sing just for me. I want this afternoon, sitting in the sun with my eyes closed and your arms around me, not able to imagine feeling more complete. But what about you? Do you want a string of girls who will give you what you ask for and nothing more, or do you want a relationship? A connection. Something *real*.'

He opened his mouth to speak, but she held up a hand to stop him. He wanted to tell her that of course he wanted all that, but how was he meant to know if that was what she really wanted too? That laying his heart out there in the open felt like asking to have someone come and smash it until there was nothing left.

'I don't want your knee-jerk reaction,' she told him. 'Whatever the answer is going to be, I need to know that you've thought about it. That you mean it.'

They sat in silence for a long minute.

'I think we both need some time,' he said eventually. 'And some space. I don't think you should come back to London,' Joe said. 'Not yet.'

Her face dropped instantly, and he knew that he had hurt her. He reached out to her and softened his expression. 'Go back to your mum. Tell her what you've told me, and make your peace with her. Make your peace with what your parents want for you, and decide, with all your cards on the table, whether it's what you want too. If it is, we'll find a way to get it for you. I'll disappear from your life if that's what you need from me.

'But if you don't…even if, with no secrets, you still want to be married to me? Come home to me, Charlie.'

CHAPTER TWELVE

CHARLIE SAT IN silence as the car sped along the roads that were so familiar to her from her childhood. She had spoken to her mother as soon as she had set off for the airport, and sensed that she wasn't entirely surprised that she was on her way back already.

She still hadn't decided what she wanted to say to her. How she would explain that she loved her parents, all her family, but that she didn't want the life that they had decided on for her.

Now the heat of the argument had faded, she could see that Joe hadn't been cruel to introduce her to his friends. The opposite, in fact. He'd shown her what she should have seen all along. Her ability to bear children or not had never been the problem—if she couldn't have kids naturally that was something that might be sad, and difficult for her and a husband to overcome. But it didn't mean that she could never have a family on her own, and it definitely wasn't a reason not to marry at all.

No, her reason for not marrying the men that her parents had introduced to her was much simpler—she didn't want them.

She didn't want the men, or the families, or the life that they represented.

She didn't want to give up her home in London, or her job, or the pride that she had built in herself and her abilities since she had left home.

She didn't want to go back to Afland just because of a promise she had made when she was eighteen and wanting to leave. Didn't want the life that she had made for herself to be over just because the date on the calendar ticked over and she was twenty-eight years old instead of twenty-seven.

Charlie bit at a nail as the car pulled through the gates of the palace and her hand barely moved from her mouth until she was in her mother's study, sitting on the other side of her expansive desk, feeling more like a job candidate than a daughter. And then she remembered that she was the one who had stalked in here and sat, leaving her mother standing on the other side of the desk, arms raised in greeting.

'So, was there something in particular you needed to talk about, sweetheart?' Adelaide asked, drawing her chair around the desk to sit beside her daughter.

Charlie felt her spine stiffen as she thought about all the things that she'd not said to her mother over the past ten years, not knowing where to start.

'I don't want to come back, Mother. After my birthday. I know I promised I would—'

'That was a long time ago,' her mother interrupted gently. 'I'd hoped that you would want to come back to live here, that your father and I might see a little more of you. But I'm not going to force you. I don't think I could if I wanted to. Now, are you going to tell me what this is really about? Is it Joe? Because we never really had a chance to talk properly before. I thought when you called after the wedding, maybe you had done something that you regretted, but then when you were here...honestly, darling, the atmosphere between you.'

Charlie couldn't help but smile when she thought of him.

'So I'm right,' her mother continued. 'You two are crazy about each other.'

'It's complicated,' Charlie said with a sigh.

'Well, I think it often is.' Her mother gave her an encouraging smile. 'Maybe if you tell me everything, it would help.'

'I wish it would, Mum. But the thing is…' She couldn't believe that she was about to volunteer the information that she'd held secret for so long, that she'd had nightmares about her mother finding out. What if she did react as she had in her dreams? Pushing her out of the family, banishing her from the island of Afland for ever? But wasn't that what Charlie had done to herself? She'd all but cut herself off from her family—her mother couldn't do any worse than that. She took a deep breath, squeezed her fingernails into her palms and spoke.

'The thing is, I might not be able to have children.' The words tumbled from her mouth in a hurry, and she kept her gaze locked on the surface of the desk, unable to meet her mother's eye.

Adelaide reached for her hand, and held it softly in her lap. 'I'm so sorry, darling. That must be terribly hard for you. And is having children important to Joe?'

'No.' She shook her head, and finally lifted her gaze to meet her mum's eyes. The gentle kindness and love on her face made a sob rise in her throat, but she forced it down, wanting to finish what she'd started. Wanting, more than anything, her mum's advice. 'He says... It doesn't matter, does it? It's not about Joe. It's about me, it's about the fact that I'm never going to be who you want me to be.'

'I just want you to be *you*, darling. And more than that, I just want you to be happy.'

But that was crap, because she'd seen for herself what her mum wanted for her. A suitable husband, marriage, babies. 'Then what was all that with Philippe?' she asked, an edge to her voice. 'Why was he talking about engagements and moving to Afland with your blessing? Why did I have to read about it in the paper?'

'Honestly, Charlie, after all this time how can you believe anything that you read? Philippe came for dinner with his parents and he asked if you were still single. You know that he'd always had a soft spot for you. Then his father asked if you were planning on moving back to Afland. I don't know where he got the rest of it from. If I know his father as well as

I think I do, the story probably came directly from him. I'm sorry that the press team weren't able to keep his mouth under control. I'm not going to lie and say that I haven't thought that you might be happier if you moved home and made a good match. It's kept your father and I happy for thirty-odd years, and your sister fairly blissful for the last seven. But we were never going to force you. Did you really think that we would?'

Yes, she had. She'd thought that there was only one way that she could make her parents happy and proud of her, but she could see from her mum's face that she'd got it wrong.

'No, I don't think you'd force me, Mum.' She stayed silent for a moment. 'I'm sorry that I've not been home much.' Her mum wrapped an arm around her shoulders. 'But seeing Verity, and the children…'

'That must have been hard.'

'I just knew that that might never happen for me, and if it doesn't then where do I fit in this family?'

Adelaide squeezed her shoulders and reached for a tissue from the silver dispenser on her desk. 'You're my little girl, Charlie. That's where you fit. Where you'll always fit. But maybe things aren't as bad as they seem. Have you seen a doctor about it?'

'Not since I first found out. I didn't want to talk about it, didn't want the press getting hold of anything.'

'Well,' Adelaide said. 'How about I set up an appointment with my personal doctor, and you can have some tests? At least then you might know where you stand. If you knew the secrets that man had kept for me...well, let's just say I know that he can be discreet.'

'And if I definitely can't have children?' Charlie asked, a shake in her voice.

'Then it won't change the way I feel about you even a tiny bit, Charlie. Surely you know that. I just want you to be happy. Is Joe making you happy?'

'He's trying. I'm trying.'

'That's good. Keep trying, both of you.'

Charlie looked up and smiled at her mum, and could see from her expression that they weren't finished yet.

'What, Mum? I know there's something else you want to say.'

'I just...I'd like to see you at home more, darling. I know that you want to stay in London. I know how important your career is. But it doesn't have to be all or nothing. You could come back to visit more. We'd love to see you. And maybe you could do a few official engagements. I can't tell you how much I've missed you.'

Charlie plugged in her headphones as she climbed into the car and cued up the tracks that Joe had sent her. They had only been apart for a night—nothing in the grand scheme of things—but the already so familiar resonance and tone of his voice managed to relax her muscles in a way she didn't know was possible. She closed her eyes as the car crept along the London streets from the airport, drumming her fingers in time to the music in her ears, remembering the morning they'd been in the music room, sitting at the piano where she'd taken lessons as a girl, next to a man who made her skin sing.

Was it pathetic that she'd broken into a smile as soon as she'd seen his name on her phone?

She tapped at the screen to bring the message up again.

Call me when you get in.

Did he mean it? Or was it just a pleasantry?

Like, *Call me when you get in, but obviously not if it's late, or inconvenient. Maybe just leave it till morning.*

Ugh. She was irritating herself, sounding like one of those pink glitter princesses she'd tried all her life not to be.

She shot off a text, the traditional middle ground between calling and not calling, telling him she'd landed and was heading back to her place. It was too much to just turn up on his doorstep, especially when she wasn't even sure that he wanted her there.

The car twisted through the darkened streets of the city, over brightly lit dual carriageways, past the twisted metal of the helter-skelter sculpture in Stratford, and on towards her flat.

Her stomach sank at the thought of another night sleeping without Joe. She told herself that a month ago she'd been perfectly happy barely aware that he existed. But that had all changed the minute that she had set eyes on him, and they couldn't change that now. Somehow, she knew that without him her flat would feel empty, even though he'd never set foot there before.

As the car approached the stuccoed, pillared front of her apartment building, she spotted a dark shadow on the front steps and her stomach lurched. She glanced back through the windshield, checking that the police officers she knew should be on her tail were there, and breathed a sigh of relief when she saw one of the officers speaking into a radio.

Just as the driver asked her over the intercom whether she wanted him to drive on, the headlights illuminated the steps, throwing light onto Joe's face, and shadows into the space behind him. She let out the breath she had been holding, and told the driver that it was fine, he could stop. She took a moment before she opened the door to gather herself, prepare for what might come with Joe.

Had he come to tell her that he wanted her? That he wanted to make this a real marriage, or that he wanted out?

'Hi,' she said as she stepped out of the car and up the steps.

'Hey,' Joe replied, giving nothing away.

She grabbed her bag from the driver and stepped past Joe, unlocking the door and pushing it open.

She reached down to grab the mail and then dumped it on the hallway table, glancing round and trying to remember what state she'd left the place in. She didn't normally care about the condition of the flat, as long as it was warm and watertight. She had spent her whole childhood and adolescence looking forward to the freedom of space that was entirely her own. But there was something selfish and lonely about that, about the fact that she didn't have to consider a single person's feelings except her own. Maybe that was why she felt irrationally pleased that the worst of the mess had been bundled into bags and carted over to Joe's place. Her flat was usually her sanctuary but today it felt cold and unloved, and for a second she thought about the warm exposed brick and softly waxed wood of Joe's warehouse and felt a pull of something like homesickness.

She shook herself as she crossed to the windows and pulled back the curtains and blinds and opened a window. It was just feeling a bit neglected in here, because she hadn't been home for a few days, she reasoned. It was nothing a bit of fresh air and the warm light of a few lamps wouldn't fix.

'Want a drink?' she called out to Joe—anything to stall actual, meaningful conversation. She grabbed them both a beer from the fridge and handed one to him.

'Nice place,' Joe said. Small talk. Good—she could handle small talk. She had plenty of formal training. Or maybe it had been bred into her. Either way, she grabbed his opening gambit and held onto it like a raft.

She chatted about the flat. How she'd chosen it for the big south-facing windows. The French doors out into the shared garden. The view of the park and lack of traffic noise from the front. She sounded like a desperate estate agent trying to close a sale.

Opening the French doors, she took her beer out to the patio, dropping onto one of the chairs and propping her knees against the edge of the little bistro table. The fairy lights her upstairs neighbour had threaded through the boughs of the trees twinkled at them, creating a scene she could have found in a fairy tale.

Shivering, she wished she'd grabbed her jacket, but she was too bone-tired to move.

'You're right, it's quiet out here,' Joe said, following her. 'Peaceful, and pretty. I can see why you like it so much.'

She looked up and met his eye, trying to judge if he was being sarcastic. But he looked genuine. He sat in the seat beside her, his thighs spread wide as he leaned back and let out a sigh.

'Long trip back,' he commented. 'For both of us.'

She 'hmm-ed' in agreement.

'Lots of time to think,' he added.

She looked up at him, wondering if this was it. When all their tiptoeing finally stopped and they decided if they wanted to run from the relationship they'd both been fighting from the first.

'Come to any conclusions?' she asked.

She wasn't sure she even wanted to know, because, whatever the answer, she knew that they still had a lot of work to do. He could declare his undying love for her this minute and that wouldn't remove a single one of the obstacles in their way. Still, even the thought of it made the hairs on her arms stand up.

'You're cold,' Joe said, stripping off his jacket and handing it to her. She draped it round her shoulders, refusing to acknowledge how delicious it felt to be wrapped in the warm, supple leather that smelt of him.

'I care about you, Charlie. I think you know that I do. But it's not as simple as that, is it?'

'I don't think that it ever is.'

'Honestly, after Arabella, and then the kiss and tell, when I'd picked myself up and convinced myself it hadn't been that bad, I thought I'd cracked it. That I'd finally figured out how these things work. And I've had no reason to doubt that I was right. What I was doing—it was working for me. Honestly, I've had no complaints.'

'So that's what—'

'Please, let me finish,' he said with a gentle smile. 'It was great, until I saw you watching me from the side of the stage in Las Vegas, and I felt something so overwhelming I still don't have the words to describe it. And I told myself that getting married was a great joke, or a killer career move or… I don't know. I told myself it was about anything except falling in love with you before I'd even said hello.'

Her heart pounded. She was desperate to say something, to ask if that was what he felt now—love. But he'd asked her for space to talk, and he deserved that.

'But I was kidding myself. I love you, Charlie. I think you knew that before I did.'

She let out the breath she had been holding, her thoughts whizzing by so fast it was impossible to concentrate on just one of them.

He sat watching her for a moment, and then grinned. 'That's it. I'm done,' he said. 'Twenty-four hours' thinking and that's all I've worked out. Say anything you like.

'Did you speak to your mum?' he asked eventually, his face falling when she couldn't think of what to say in response.

She nodded, still searching for the words. 'It was good,' she said eventually. 'I think…I think I got a lot of things wrong.'

'About me?'

She smiled, tempted to call him out on his self-centredness that only a rock star could get away with.

'About family, about children, about myself.' She looked up and met his eye. 'Yes, probably a few things wrong about you too.' She sighed, knowing that she was going to have to dig deeper than that. For so long, she'd kept as much as she could get away with to herself, but Joe deserved more than that from her.

'I'm not going back, to Afland. Well, not properly. I told my mum I'd take on some official duties, but my life will be here, Joe. I'm staying in London. And I hope to God that it's with you, because I've missed you like…

I don't know. Like I suddenly lost my hearing and there was no music in the world.'

Now it was her turn to squirm, looking into her man's eyes as she waited for him to reply. 'Is that what you want, Joe?'

'I want you, Charlie. Any way I can have you. Is that enough?'

She leaned forwards and pressed a hard kiss against his lips, gasping with pleasure as his hands wound around her waist under the warm leather of his jacket. 'It's enough,' she managed to whisper between kisses. 'We can make it enough—if we both want it.' His arms pulled tighter around her waist and she moved away from him for just a split second, and then she was sitting on top of him, her legs straddled around him and the chair. He leaned back, meeting her eyes as she settled on top of him. 'We're doing this?' he asked.

She answered him with a kiss.

EPILOGUE

'YOU KNOW, YOU HAVEN'T said it,' Joe said sleepily, brushing a strand of her hair back from her shoulder. He pulled the duvet up around them and Charlie in close, settling her in the crook of his arm as he laid his head on the pillow.

'Said what?'

Her eyes were shut, her body loose and languid, and her voice so sleepy she barely formed words.

'You know what.'

She opened her eyes and looked up at him, a teasing smile on her lips. 'I can't say it now that you've asked.'

Joe pressed a kiss into her hair. 'I don't need you to. But, you know, tomorrow, if you happened to feel the urge…'

'I predict lots of urges, tomorrow.' She smiled wickedly. 'It's a long, long list. But if that's the one that you want to put at the top…'

If he'd had any energy left, he would have rolled on top of her and taken care of a few of those urges right now. But instead he pinched her waist. 'Give me an hour's sleep and I'll put myself entirely in your hands.'

'Good. Exactly where I want you. Later,' she said, with another kiss against his chest. 'I think there's something we need to talk about first.'

He sighed sleepily. 'I thought we were done talking.'

She shuffled away from him on the bed, pulling up the sheets to try and find some modesty.

'It's important, Joe,' she said, and he opened his eyes properly at the serious tone of her voice. 'There's a lot we didn't talk about. Children for one. It's not a fun conversation, but we have to have it. I'm going to see my mum's doctor, but there are no guarantees. What if it never happens for us?'

He rubbed his face and sat up. 'If it comes to that, Charlie, we'll deal with it. Together. There are other ways to have a family.'

'Is it what you want?' she asked, a wobble in her voice. 'Because I don't know if adoption is something that I could take on. With my family, the succession, it's complicated.'

He kissed her on the forehead, smoothing

a hand down her spine. 'I know that. But no, it doesn't matter to me. You're what matters to me.'

'But I might never have a family, Joe. And there's no point taking this any further if that's not something that you can live with. If you're always going to want more.'

He stopped her with a kiss on the lips. 'The only thing I want in my future is you,' he said, between kisses. 'We're going to travel the world. We're going to make beautiful music. We're going to party until we can't take any more. If children come along, the more the merrier. But nothing, *nothing* is going to make me a happier man than knowing that you will come home with me every night, and wake up with me every morning.'

'I love you,' she whispered, and he smiled as he squeezed her tight and pressed a kiss against her hair. She ran her hands over his chest, and he stretched, bringing their bodies into contact from where she had propped herself on his chest right down to their toes.

'And I love you too. Now, are we making a start on that list of yours?'

* * * * *

If you really enjoyed this story, check out
NEWBORN ON HER DOORSTEP
by Ellie Darkins.
Available now!

If you're looking forward to another
royal romance read, you won't want to miss
MARRIED FOR HIS SECRET HEIR
by Jennifer Faye.

COMING NEXT MONTH FROM

HARLEQUIN®

Romance

Available June 6, 2017

#4571 HER PREGNANCY BOMBSHELL

Summer at Villa Rosa • by Liz Fielding

Pilot Miranda Marlowe is pregnant with her widower boss's baby! And so she's heading for the beautiful Mediterranean island palazzo Villa Rosa. Cleve Finch knows he must make things right with the woman who's kiss he can't forget, but will his marriage proposal convince her of his love for her—and their unborn baby?

#4572 MARRIED FOR HIS SECRET HEIR

Mirraccino Marriages • by Jennifer Faye

Earl Luca DiSalvo and Elena Ricci have one magical evening in Paris... with dramatic consequences! Luca is reluctant to marry, but when beautiful Elena reveals her baby secret, his royal duty means he has no choice—he must get down on one knee and make her his wife!

#4573 BEHIND THE BILLIONAIRE'S GUARDED HEART

by Leah Ashton

Reclusive billionaire Hugh Bennell likes his life—and his emotions—uncomplicated, but meeting glamorous heiress April Molyneux changes everything. Hugh doesn't do relationships, and April wants to keep the independence she's worked so hard for. But with these sparks flying...resistance might be futile!

#4574 A MARRIAGE WORTH SAVING

by Therese Beharrie

Leaving his ex-wife, Mila, was the hardest thing that Jordan Thomas has ever had to do. But when fate brings them back together, he's reminded of what drew him to his beautiful wife in the first place, and he wonders...is it *ever* too late for a second chance?

YOU CAN FIND MORE INFORMATION ON UPCOMING HARLEQUIN® TITLES, FREE EXCERPTS AND MORE AT WWW.HARLEQUIN.COM.

HRLPCNM0517

Miranda Marlowe has just discovered she's pregnant with her boss's baby...

Read on for a sneak preview of
HER PREGNANCY BOMBSHELL

Tomorrow she would go down to the beach, feel the sand beneath her feet, let the cold water of the Mediterranean run over her toes. Then, like an old lady, she would go and lie up to her neck in a rock pool heated by the hot spring and let its warmth melt away the confused mix of feelings, the desperate hope that she would turn around, Cleve would be there and, somehow, everything would be back to normal.

It wasn't going to happen and she wasn't going to burden Cleve with this.

She'd known what she was doing when she'd chosen to see him through a crisis in the only way she knew how.

She'd seen him at his weakest, broken, weeping for all that he'd lost, and she'd left before he woke so that he wouldn't have to face her. Struggle to find something to talk about over breakfast.

She'd known that there was only ever going to be one end to the night they'd spent together. One of them would have to walk away and it couldn't be Cleve.

HREXP0517

Four weeks ago she was an experienced pilot working for Goldfinch Air Services, a rapidly expanding air charter and freight company. She could have called any number of contacts and walked into another job.

Three weeks and six days ago she'd spent a night with the boss and she was about to become a cliché. Pregnant, single and grounded.

She'd told the border official that she was running away and she was, but not from a future in which there would be two of them. The baby she was carrying was a gift. She was running away from telling Cleve that she was pregnant.

She needed to sort out exactly what she was going to do, have a plan firmly in place, everything settled, so that when she told him the news he understood that she expected nothing. That he need do nothing…

HREXP0517